Firefly: The Half-Blood Angel

FIREFLY:

THE HALF-BLOOD ANGEL

THE GUARDIANS OF LIGHT SERIES
BOOK THREE

Kasey Hill

Azoth Khem Publishing
Huntsville, AL
April 2025

AZOTH KHEM

© Azoth Khem Publishing, 2025

ISBN: 978-1-952880-25-4
First Edition 2020
Second Edition 2025

Azoth Khem Publishing
29931 Copperpenny Drive NW
Harvest, AL 35749
www.azothkhem.com

Ordering Information:
Quantity sales and exclusive discounts are available on quantity
purchases by corporations, associations, and others. For details,
contact the publisher at the address above. For orders by U.S. trade
bookstores and wholesalers, please contact
Azoth Khem Publishing: Tel: (256) 221-5498 or visit
www.azothkhem.com

Printed in the United States of America

For my Luxina

Check out these other series by Kasey Hill

The Guardians of Light Series
Firefly of Immortality
The Shining Ones
Firefly: The Half-Blood Angel
The Valley of the Shadow of Death: Nephilim
Rising

Dark Woods Series
Devil's Claw

The Whispering Spirits Series
The Haunting at Foxwood Village
Dark Coven

Coming Soon to The Guardians of Light
Series
Firefly of Immortality II
Black Wings of Death
Firefly of Immortality: Anniel Unveiled
Alpha and Omega
Firefly of the Apocalypse

Coming Soon to The Guardians of Light
Series Universe

The Guardians of Light: Darkness Falls Series
Bloodlines: Into the Shadows

Firefly: The Half-Blood Angel

CHAPTER 1

I HAVE A SECRET. Secrets are something hard to keep. I was a secret that came to light. My mother had an affair with my father, and here I am. However, that's old news. Water under the bridge, so to speak. I never came to know nor love my mother and father. I came to love Alpha as my sole parent. But love is a fickle thing. It can come and go as it pleases, and now, I hold nothing more than loathing and apathy toward Alpha. Whether he knows it to be true is undoubtedly the question. Still, that is not my secret, either. My secret is simple. I am not evil.

I have done horrible things in the name of Alpha. I didn't care. I had no one else to guide me, and I felt that he was guiding me in a way I needed to go. His rhetoric, his law, seemed right and true. I was his little monster, and I enjoyed it. However, I came to learn he was hiding something from me, something that would change my life forever.

I grew up abnormally because I, myself, was not a typical angel. My mother was special, like her twin soul, and they held powers not seen in any other angel ever created by Alpha and Omega. I had no guidance, and Alpha knew only to use those powers for his own gain. For those differences, I did not age the same as other angels would. I aged expediently into my late teens, where it halted. That was when the more challenging training came, and I found myself forced into training even when I did not want it. Alpha had his reason but never divulged it to me. I found out later. I found out when he swept me away and told me we had to leave the Summit. The Fallen Angels were revolting and reclaiming their places in the purified world he had created. Most believed his actions for requesting someone to oppose him was to create a balance in the world. It was not. He needed to eliminate those who were poisoned and would not follow him to the end with his plans. Those who chose to fall with Omega were the poison, and those left behind were the pure. It was a culling, so to speak. He believed those who remained behind were loyal to him and none other. He was wrong.

There were active members of his angel fleet who were working with those who fell to return them to the Summit. My mother and father were among those angels. Ultimately, in the end, they fell as well to join Omega in her war against Alpha. Even with all of this, I was still Alpha's loyal little soldier. It would be years later that I found out a piece of information that sent my blood to boil. I had siblings that Alpha never told me about.

I had come to learn that I dream, and angels do not dream. At least, typical angels do not. I was far beyond normal. It was within these dreams that I found my siblings. It was always the same place. There was a field in the middle of nowhere with a tree at the center. It was so peaceful and serene. I had been walking these fields for years until, to my surprise, two others joined the place. I hid away from them, envious of their connection. I learned their names while there: Luxina and Xavier. There were times I had nearly come out of my hiding spot to introduce myself to them, to get to know them, but I was cowardly. They hardly knew about each other except in their dreams, and even then, they only knew each other's names. They did not know they were born as twin flames like their mother and father were. So, I sat, and I watched them from afar. I grew fond of them both.

To my horror, Alpha had gained the ability to spy on my dreams along with me. It was then that he became something different. He became distant and malevolent. He locked himself away from me, and it was then I realized I had no one. We had been hiding out in the old Chernobyl buildings, long ago abandoned. I had no idea he was inventing a new race, a new breed of angel. And it was going to start with me.

I traveled with him to the Unseelie Court, where Queen Mab gazed upon me in amazement and desire. She listened to Alpha as he wagered with her, never removing her eyes from me.

"I will give you what you want on two conditions," she replied as Alpha stood by eagerly waiting for her demands. "The first one will be that if you are to succeed, I get to keep this one as my payment," she said, motioning her eyes to me and smiling deviously.

"What is your second condition?" Alpha asked.

Her smile grew wider and even more sinister. "My second condition is if you fail, you yourself will become a prisoner of my court. You may never leave, and you will lose all godly powers you have ever gained. You will, of course, be very well taken care of. However, you pose a threat to all. You have two years to complete the trials."

"That is ludicrous. I would never wager myself for power. You would have to be a fool to strike such a deal," Alpha huffed.

"Well, then you don't get what you came for," Mab replied, holding up a vial of blood. "This is what you wanted, of course, right? A vial of pure blood. My blood?"

Alpha stared at the vile as his face twitched and darkened.

"This could be yours if you are willing to pay the price," she said, twisting the vile back and forth, almost as if she were enchanting Alpha.

"You have no authority over me," Alpha stated. "What makes you think I wouldn't destroy you here and now for the endless amount of blood to gain from your dripping carcass!"

"You cannot harm me," she replied, raising an eyebrow and grinning. "I am older than you and was made by gods that ensured I could never be harmed by gods lower on the spectrum than what they were. Try all you might, you will die before ever touching a hair on my head."

Alpha gulped. I had silently stood by, watching the two of them bicker back and forth. Free of Alpha sounded like a blessing. If he failed, I would be free of his tyranny. Free.

The Dark Queen glanced in my direction as if I had spoken it aloud. I looked around in terror, hoping Alpha had not heard either.

Do not fear, my little Shining One. He cannot hear you as I can.

I was a bit fearful and shocked. I looked at Alpha, who was lost in thought while making his decision.

I can hear you, too? I asked.

Of course, young Damian. You have special gifts like your mother, your brother, and your sister. You have an enchantment that needs finished sealing, however. You need to escape Alpha and find your brother and sister and join them on their quest. Together, all three of you will be able to save the world, she replied.

What quest? They haven't even met yet, I replied.

All in due time, young one.

"My patience is growing thin, Alpha," Mab seethed. "What shall it be?"

Alpha spoke finally. "I will agree to your conditions."

The Dark Queen laughed maniacally, turned over an hourglass, and looked back at Alpha. "Tick tock, Alpha."

Since that meeting, I have been tortured with various injections. The Dark Queen did not tell him it would be harder for my blood to adhere to the magic since I was not wholly a Shining One. And there were dangers if it did succeed. I may become something completely evil like those vile creatures he had created in the beginning. I didn't want that. But I had no one to stop him from trying them on me.

I lay in agony for days after the first series of injections he created. Hell wasn't even a description that could bring the pain I felt justice. My body rejected injection after injection. With each injection, he would lock himself away, trying to perfect the serum using as little of Queen Mab's blood as he could. He synthesized it to make it last longer. I came to learn that I was not the only one he was using them on as well. He had been taking lower demons created by the Forsaken and experimenting with them as well. They were once humans with just a trace of angelic blood in their systems. Many died at the hands of Alpha. But he didn't care. He wanted this, and whatever Alpha wanted, Alpha received.

I never wanted to be a test dummy. They had to drag me, kicking and screaming, to the chamber to be administered the injections. I fought with everything I had. I froze some of those who dragged me away with my freezing ability. I fought many off in sword combat, killing many of them. I was always outnumbered and always subdued. After so many times of trying to fight, my spirit broke. I eventually began to allow them to lead me to the testing chamber. They would shackle me to a bed while I endured the burning lava injections. Quite a few times, I came close to death, and I begged for mercy to feel the cooling feeling of the abyss envelop me and carry me off to the angel's potter's field. I always recovered at the last minute and would cry for days after wondering what I had done to deserve everything I endured.

The only thing that kept me going and kept me fighting to survive was Luxina and Xavier. I had to keep them from Alpha's grips, even if it meant I was subject to his torturous methods. I knew one day we would be able to meet and greet. I could get to know the family I never had growing up. And I would kill anyone that tried to hurt them.

My only solace and escape were my dreams, where I got to see them. If I could see them, I knew they were safe. They had yet to meet as well and only graced each other in their dreams. The first time I saw them, the power they emitted upon touching each other's hand was monumental. I envied their connection, but I was not jealous of them. They were perfect together. Alpha, at one point, wanted me to do what he had done with Sophie and Incaendiel for all of those years. He wanted me to get Luxina to try and love me, severing her connection with Xavier and becoming less powerful. That's where the twin flames gain their strength, with the connection with their twin soul. I would never do that. I could never do that. However, everyone thinks I am an evil little sentinel for Alpha. If it keeps everyone else I love safe from Alpha, I will let them think that until the day I die.

I remember the day that Lucifer finally made it to Alpha. He didn't even fight his way here. He found one of the sentinels of the Forsaken and bartered his way here, promising Alpha Luxina and Xavier in exchange for me. I immediately hated him. I stood by Alpha's side and glared at him with all of the hate in the world as he proposed to bring Xavier first and then Luxina for Alpha's disposal. All the while, Alpha listened, never intending to let him have me in return. I tried to stop them. I disguised myself and tried to interfere before it was too late. I pretended to be one of the hunting pack that looked for me days on end. That's when I met my mother. I may not think of her much as a mother because I wasn't raised by her, but I could see the good in her heart and the love she had for me.

There were times I would go back to the Summit with them and would watch how she interacted with Xavier, and it made me hate myself. She sacrificed the love for her one son to find the one that was hopeless. Xavier suffered at my expense. Whenever I would catch Sophie alone, we would talk about how much she adored Xavier and also how much he despised her. He felt abandoned by her in her pursuit of finding me. It was I who convinced her to stop searching and return to the Summit to be with Xavier. She needed to protect him from Lucifer because the plan was drawing to a close. If I had acted sooner than later in convincing her to go back and give up, he would not have been harmed by Alpha. There would have been ample time to hide him away. The day came for Lucifer to steal Xavier away, and there wasn't anything I could do to save him without exploiting myself.

I watched as he put our mother in the tower like Alpha had done so many times. It was the same tower I had been born in that he and Sophie were held prisoner in. I already had plans on breaking them out long before Luxina arrived in Chernobyl. What I wasn't expecting was them to dose me along with the others. It made me weak and vulnerable. I had to listen to what I was told without exception. The mind control substance he gave me bent me in ways I couldn't escape until it wore off. I met Xavier long before Luxina arrived, and he already had a steady hate for me. Why wouldn't he hate me? I was the reason he grew up without a mother. She was always looking for me instead of being by his side. I would hate me, too. Our first encounter was less than astounding and not at all what I had imagined meeting my brother for the first time. His pure hatred for me made me falter each time I was in his presence. At times, the injections broke me, and I found myself at his throat, trying to kill him as he egged me on with his venomous words. There would be no doubt that if given the chance to kill me, he would try with all of his might. He had no compassion, just as I didn't. Again, something that can be laid to rest on my shoulders.

When Lucifer came to Alpha ready to go in for Luxina, I wanted to head the party that brought her in. I wanted to keep her as safe as possible. Alpha agreed to let me go, but not before another one of his cocktail injections. I remember slapping her at some point and felt terrible after the injection began to taper off. She was held for a few days before Alpha brought her to his office to meet with her. I expected her to hate me, but I could feel the sorrow and compassion leach from her to me. She wanted to save me. She wanted to truly save me and everyone from the clutches of Alpha. I remember how her heart sank as we walked through the halls, and she heard the cries of the creatures Alpha had been running experiments on. He would inject them, morph them, take their blood after it mutated, and then kill them if they weren't of any use to him.

I witnessed her defiance in front of Alpha when he asked her to join his side. I had heard so many stories of Incaendiel when it came to Alpha, and it was one of the few moments I was glad she had her father's temper and spirit. She would need it to survive the injection. The ones he gave me were vastly different than the ones he had planned to use on her. Even the ones Xavier was subjected to were different than the ones she had. She was receiving almost pure blood from Mab and a cocktail mix of all of the mutt creations he had made.

I watched the moment she struck a nerve in him, and at the last minute, he added an injection that I was unaware of what the contents were. That was until he injected her with them all. He had created an injection that he called Heavenly Hellfire. He gave it to those who refused to cooperate with him. It must have been one of the injections he gave me in the beginning but twice the dose. He could bend the mind to his will through the injections. He wasn't counting on her defiance being even stronger than the injections.

When the Heavenly Hellfire failed, he gave her a series of injections to kill her. Her will to live was just as strong as her defiance. I watched her writhe in agony, and they just kept the injections coming. When I tried to help, when I tried to stave them off from injecting any more of the serum into her, they caught me in the neck with one. It burned through my body, searing every nerve ending I had. I reached out to Xavier with my mind before they pulled me out of the room.

Get her to Stygia. Find Sophia. Quick, before she dies. She will be the only one to end this war, and Alpha's reign of terror will come to an end. I will find you, and we will stop him together.

A flicker of acknowledgement rolled across Xavier's face, and I watched through the window of the closing door behind me as he broke the chains free from the wall and swooped her from the place to safety. I, however, was unable to escape to help them. Instead, I was subjected to beatings and torture. I had injections over and over until my body had gone numb and my soul had gone limp.

There was hardly any fight left in me. All I could do was think over and over that Xavier had made it to Stygia in time to save Luxina.

I sent him to Sophia for a very specific reason. She knew what to tell them. She knew what to explain to them about what we were. I had come across her once before, and we began to meet in private. She had a plan to help thwart Alpha, but it wouldn't work unless all of the Shining Ones were together. She herself had been to see Mab and knew more things than I could imagine about what we were. We were more than just meager angels. We were almost gods, and together, we were more powerful than Alpha.

It had been several days after Xavier and Luxina had escaped that Alpha came to me in the dungeon. I was chained to the ceiling, suspended off the ground to where my tip toes just barely grazed the floor. He watched me as I spat blood from my mouth. I had just recently been tossed around the room, and my wounds were still fresh.

"You disappointed me, son." His words fell flat as he pulled a chair up and sat down in it. "You helped them escape, and I know you did. What I don't know is how? And most importantly, why? Why is my best soldier turning against me? I raised you. I gave you everything you could ever want. And this is how you repay me. You throw it back in my face!"

He composed himself and watched for my reaction. I gave him absolutely nothing.

"I have half a mind to feed you to those mutts starving in the cell across from you, but I need you, unfortunately. You have one more chance to prove yourself worthy of me. You will be going along with Lucifer and me to Stygia to get your siblings back. I need all of you together. Are you going to follow my wishes, or are you going just to hang here until your body gives out?" he asked.

I quickly ran everything through my mind. I had to go along. I had to help them escape before he could recapture them. There was no choice.

"I will go with you," I replied.

"Excuse me?" he asked indignantly.

"I will go with you, *father*," I replied once more, emphasizing father for him.

He looked pleased with himself and made a motion with his two forefingers. Asmodeus emerged from the shadows and walked toward me. He released a lever from the wall, and my chain came bounding down from the ceiling. My legs were so weak that I hit the ground with a thud. I could barely feel any of the muscles in my body. Asmodeus walked over and unshackled by bound wrists.

You need to run as soon as you can. Alpha will kill you if this plan falls through, he thought.

I had no idea he knew I could read his thoughts, or anyone knew for that matter. I acknowledged him with my eyes as Alpha watched us. He pulled the chains from around me that had landed in a heap on my legs. I shakily stood stretching out my still numb limbs.

"Mark my words, boy. You fail me and do not kill who I tell you to kill... Well, you can imagine the rest," Alpha stated, turning on his heels, and left the dungeon room with Asmodeus close behind. "We leave at dawn."

I spent all night trying to devise a plan for Xavier and Luxina to escape safely. I hated the thought of having to kill others to protect them, but I have to act like I am on Alpha's side, or else they won't have anyone to help them any longer. I cleaned up all of my cuts and applied a poultice to my bruises when I was back in my room. I winced with each touch as the cuts burned with the herbs.

My door opened, and I thought it was probably Lucifer coming to check on me. However, it was not Lucifer. It was the last person I ever thought I would see walk through that door. It was my mother, Sophie. She ran to my side and threw her arms around me.

"My boy, my sweet, precious boy," she murmured through silent tears of joy.

I winced with pain as she squeezed my broken ribs.

"What have they done to you?" she asked, looking me over and fretting.

She picked up the salve I had been applying and began to gingerly treat my wounds as I stood there in both shock and disbelief. Her fingers worked nimbly over each of the wounds I had until they reached my face. She stopped short and just stared into my eyes as I stared back.

"What are you doing here?" I asked, still confused as to what I was seeing.

She set the jar of salve down on the table, pulled a chair out, and sat down, clasping her hands while leaning forward.

"Alpha attacked the Glade, where a fleet of angels were set up planning an attack to get Luxina and Xavier back," she began. "Before the mountain fully fell, I was grabbed and whisked away to here by Lucifer. He told me he had you three here together all safe."

"Why haven't I seen you before today then?" I asked, stretching a shirt over my head.

"I wanted to see all of you. I wanted to rescue all of you. However, I was chained in a room until I could prove that I wasn't here to stop Alpha. I agreed that it would be safer for all three of you to stay with Alpha than risk trying to take you from here without any help," she explained.

"So, you stood by while they gave Luxina injections? How long has it been since you have been here? Were you here when Xavier was receiving his injections as well? Why didn't you stop them?!" I seethed.

"I was not here for the injections Xavier received. And I was receiving them myself when Luxina arrived," she replied softly. "When Luxina failed to bow to Alpha during his head games, he doubled my doses of Heavenly Hellfire. I made a connection with Luxina and may have said things that were... not truthful to her. I blamed her for my current predicament. The child I had yet to meet, and I was cursing her for defying the one person we all defied after the fall."

Sophie looked away, ashamed.

"I could hear Incaendiel calling out her name to pull her out of that nightmarish place we were stuck together in," she said as she began to weep again. "I said horrible things to him as well prior to the Glade coming down. I'm not even sure if anyone knows I am alive."

I ran my hand through my hair, frustrated.

"Why are you here?" I asked again heatedly.

"I just told you—"

"No, why are you in my room?" I yelled. "Did you think you could come in here and just sweet-talk your way into me calling you mother and collapsing in your arms in tears because you had finally saved me from the evil monster I have called father since I was little?"

She looked a bit stunned at my choice of words.

"My brother and sister are being hunted down like wild animals, and you're sitting here playing tea party with Alpha instead of helping them. You're a terrible excuse for a mother, and you are no mother to me. Please, leave my room," I ordered, pointing in the direction of the door.

"But, I thought," she began, confused. "You don't want to be taken from Alpha?" she asked.

"Not at the risk of my brother and sister falling into his clutches again. They are more important than me. What kind of brother would I be to allow them back here to be tortured more by that devil in disguise? I would be no better than you or Lucifer."

I stared at her long and hard.

"Lucifer," she started when I cut her off again.

"Don't get me started about that pathetic waste of space. You're honestly going to sit there and defend him when he was the one that orchestrated the entire kidnapping plot of both of your children. I am not more important than two lives." I held my door open for her to leave. I looked her dead in the eyes and said, "You will never be my mother, and Lucifer will never be my father. I don't have a family. Had it been my decision, you would have died in that mountain."

Dumbfounded, she just gave me a nod and left the room. I slammed the door closed behind her and threw myself backward on my bed, landing on my back. I would never understand her rhetoric of thinking. Had she been totally brainwashed? I stared at the ceiling for quite some time before another knock came on my door.

"For the love of all that is holy," I muttered, standing to answer the knock.

I opened the door, and yet another face I despised stood before me. Lilith, Omega, whatever you want to call her, loomed in the doorway before letting herself in the room. She walked around the room, lifting things up and setting them back down. I watched her, completely unaware of what she was trying to accomplish. She unscrewed the lightbulb in the room, and once she was satisfied with whatever search she was doing, she sat down in the chair my mother had just left not too long ago.

"Hello, Damian. We have yet to formally meet," she stated after a moment of silence.

"I'm Damian. You're Lilith. We have met now, so you can leave," I replied hastily, motioning to the door.

She studied me with eyes that were unfamiliar. A glimmer of life floated through her eyes before they glazed back over. She swallowed, slightly clearing her throat before she spoke to me again.

"When you leave to go with Alpha on this trip, you must escape him once Xavier and Luxina are safe," she declared, unwavering in her lack of emotion.

"I already know. He plans to kill me if his plan fails," I replied, annoyed.

"You could only wish for death for what he has planned for you after it fails," she whispered.

"I just spent days being strung up by my arms with my feet barely touching the ground to stand up. I'm sure whatever it is, I can handle it," I retorted.

"You have such a fighting spirit. If I didn't know any better, I would swear your father was Incaendiel instead of the lousy one that brought you forth," she remarked, fire blazing in her eyes.

"That is something I can agree with," I replied with a wicked grin. "My father is a piece of crap that deserves nothing more than to be doused in gasoline and dropped into the lake of fire."

"Now, since we are on the same page," she decreed, careening her neck and smiling, "let's get down to the matter at hand. All three of you need to be as far away from Alpha as possible after this raid ends. Unless you can absolutely convince him that you had nothing to do with their escape... "

"I don't know how many times I have to stress to you people that I don't care what Alpha does to me as long as Xavier and Luxina are safe," I barked, exasperated. "I hate repeating myself over and over."

"For the power of the Shining Ones to work, to put an end to Alpha, all three of you have to be together," Lilith urged. "You weren't supposed to have become. I never imagined that Sophie would succumb to weakness in that tower. So, when Luxina and Xavier were born, they were not born with the full power they should have had. You are the missing piece in all of that. You have to make it to them and join them. Or else, all of this will have been for naught."

"If I wasn't supposed to exist, I wouldn't," I snarled. "What makes you so sure it's me that wasn't supposed to exist and not one of them?"

She eyed me, pursing her lips. I could see I struck a nerve. Everyone knew about how my mother had me and what she did. She had betrayed Incaendiel. So, most think I wasn't supposed to exist because of that. Had Sophie never been in the tower with Lucifer, I wouldn't exist here because she would have never been tempted. However, it doesn't say anywhere that twin souls have to be born at the same time, so it is quite possible that I am supposed to be and Xavier not. However, either way, it doesn't change anything. I will protect him either way.

"Why are you helping us when you are joining forces with Alpha?" I asked suspiciously.

"Because out of everything I have made in this world, Sophia and Incaendiel will be the one thing I cherish the most. In extension, you three are also my cherished creations. I will not see my creations destroyed. If it comes down to it, Alpha will have to destroy me in the end and then figure out how to rebuild the universe alone. I have never stopped loving Alpha. He is my other half no matter how screwed up he is. It was inevitable for us to come back together."

"What do you suggest I do then?" I asked.

"What we all have been telling you to. Run."

CHAPTER 2

ALPHA ASSEMBLED an army to raid Stygia. Every demon was armed with a sword and instructed to kill anyone who attempted to interfere. The Shining Ones, Xavier and Luxina, were to remain unharmed. If Incaendiel happened to be there, he was to be taken alive as well. Lucifer and I were to head the mission, and Alpha came along to observe. As we waited for the rest of the soldiers to fall in line, Lucifer tried to make small talk with me.

"Your mother told me she came in and saw you last night," he lamented, loading himself down with weapons.

"Yup," I replied curtly.

"She said it was groundbreaking," he raved.

"I'm sure for her it was," I snidely retorted.

"Everything we do, we do for you, Damian," Lucifer reasoned.

"I'm sure you do everything for me and not for

yourself," I returned curtly.

"One day you will see," he stressed, falling off from his sentence.

"One day you will see what a piece of-"

"Fall in, soldiers!" Alpha commanded.

I glared and repositioned my chest armor. Everyone else readied themselves.

"Off we go!" Alpha ordered.

He was seated in a chariot pulled by four horses. A red one, a black one, a white one, and a pale gray one pulled him along like he was the antichrist himself. His chariot shot off into the air, and we all lifted up in flight alongside him. It didn't take us long to make it to the entrance. That was the one beautiful thing about flying. You could get anywhere you wanted in the blink of an eye. I'm sure we looked like we were flying into the apocalypse had we been seen by others heading toward Stygia. Alpha must make a grand entrance wherever he goes. It's quite nauseating as opposed to get in and get out, getting the job done without showboating victory.

I found it odd that there were no guards standing to prevent us from entering. Were we walking into a trap? Alpha paid no mind to the fact there wasn't anyone guarding the place and marched right in. No sooner had we breached the entrance than alarms sounded, echoing throughout the underground facility. We watched as they all scrambled into their positions. The demon fleet began their assault on those that made an appearance and soon were fighting their way through the Watchers. Lucifer, Alpha, and I broke off into one of the side tunnels. I had no idea where we were going when the fighting was taking place in the main corridors.

"Do you know where she would go?" Alpha asked Lucifer.

"She has her own private quarters. We just must follow this path and go through the maze. I know the way there. I have visited her a few times," Lucifer replied.

"Good. She will surely be the one to hide them and send them off to safety," Alpha droned.

"Who?" I asked, unsure if my gut was tugging me toward the right answer.

"Sophia, of course," Alpha proclaimed.

Oh no. Not Sophia. We followed Lucifer through the maze of tunnels below. He weaved through them as if he had been here more than just a few times. He seemed to know them like the back of his hand. How long had he been seeing Sophia? Did he know that she had filled me in on details in prior meetings? I know Sophia was his bound soulmate who left the Summit long after the Fallen Ones had chosen to side with Lilith. Had he been still coming to see her even after declaring my mother as his true love? If he had been, it would have been pretty crappy on his part. As much as I dislike Sophie for her errors in judgement calls and choices she has made regarding Luxina and Xavier, she didn't deserve that type of treatment.

We arrived at the door that Lucifer said would be her quarters. I expected Lucifer to break the door in himself, however, that was not the case.

"Damian, you go in first," Alpha requested.

I knew it was not a request, but moreover a demand of compliance. I nodded my acknowledgement of his request and busted through the door. I caught a glimpse of her putting the rug down just in time over the escape hatch in the floor. They were safe for the time being. I held my breath, hoping that neither Lucifer nor Alpha had seen what I had.

"Where are they, Sophia?" Lucifer demanded.

I let out a sigh of relief by mistake and then looked to see if either had been watching me. Alpha eyed me curiously, but he didn't say a word.

"You will never find them, love," she replied.

"Oh, but you are mistaken, dear Sophia," Alpha decreed.

"Let the other child go, Alpha. You are going to kill him with your experiments," she hissed.

"Oh, I beg to differ. It seems as if the last injection has held out far longer than any other I have given him. Pretty soon, I will make a permanent one and bend you all to my will!" he exclaimed.

"Damian, come here, son," Lucifer called.

I had to keep my composure even though my blood boiled just at the mere thought of having to acknowledge him calling me son without refuting it.

"Yes, Lucifer," I replied.

"Kill everyone in this room, especially her," Lucifer spat.

"Let's go look for the other two," Alpha said. "They can't have gotten far."

As they left the room, I spoke silently to Sophia.

I was going to use this opportunity to escape, but now I can't. I'm not going to hurt you; just play along, ok?

She nodded.

I'm sorry, but I have to kill them, I motioned to the Watchers standing in the corner.

Do what you must, she replied.

I watched as they laid their swords down and sacrificed themselves for the cause. I made their deaths swift, and it broke my heart knowing that there were so many that would die for this cause.

"Damian, you don't have to listen to them. You don't have to do this!" Sophia pleaded.

"Scream," I said.

She let out a bloodcurdling scream, and I smeared blood all over her from the others I had slain. She lay still on the floor in case anyone came in to do body checks. I had lost my opportunity to run by saving her. Had I not done what I did, they would have found Xavier and Luxina by following me. I walked from the room with blood splattered all over me and caught up to Lucifer and Alpha ahead in the cavern. I hoped my plan worked, or else I would be the body lying in blood on the floor when Alpha got done with me.

"Well done, son," Alpha remarked, patting me on the back.

We made our way back to the main cave entrance, and bodies lay mangled everywhere. Demons stood around chattering while others were scouring the rest of the cavern to see if there were others that had not escaped yet to slay. There was one person that stood hooded with their hands bound behind their back. Asmodeus held him firmly by the shoulders.

"We found Incaendiel, sir," Asmodeus stated.

"Good, that means the kids aren't too far gone. I want this place searched top to bottom. Every person alive I want questioned until death succumbs them. I want those two found and brought to me. That's an order!" Alpha bellowed.

"What do we do with him?" Asmodeus asked, nudging Incaendiel.

"Damian, escort our fearless leader here back to our quarters. We have much to discuss, Incaendiel and I," Alpha demanded.

"Yes, sir," I replied.

Asmodeus handed Incaendiel over to me, and I

blinked him into the very dungeon they had held me. I placed the shackles tied to the wall on his wrists before I cut the ropes away from his hands. I removed his hood, and all he did was glare at me. Thousands of thoughts swirled through his head. *Where were Luxina and Xavier? Where was Sophia? How many were dead? How can I kill him and escape out of here?*

"They're safe and will stay safe," I whispered.

His face contorted in a confused, angry glare.

I looked around to make sure we were still alone. "We will talk more later," I assured him as I left the dungeon.

Just as I closed the door, Alpha appeared before me.

"The prisoner is secured," I reported.

"Good, good," he replied.

He studied me long and hard. I didn't know if I was dismissed or if I was required to stand there until he walked away.

"You did good today, my boy," he praised, clapping his hand on my shoulder. "Return to your living quarters and await further instruction."

"Yes, sir," I replied and brushed past him as fast as I could.

I didn't like how he was studying me lately. I felt insecure, as if my poker face was going to break. I believe my face may have shown some flicker of guilt at some point by the way he had been watching me and surveying my actions closer than usual. It wasn't much longer after I had made it back to my room that four of Alpha's lackeys busted in and dragged me off to the injection chamber. I kicked and lashed out the best I could. I caught one of them in the eye with my fist and another in the mouth with my foot. They never would take me without a fight.

"I did what I was told! I killed without thought!" I screamed as they tossed me onto the metal table and locked me into place. "Why?!"

"Because you failed the mission," Alpha replied, walking into the room and holding the injection himself.

"I killed. I brought Incaendiel back here like you asked. What more could you want from me?!" I spat.

"The twins were not secured," Alpha lectured monotonously.

"They were gone when we got there!" I protested. "There wasn't any way for me to find them with the tasks you had given me!"

"I do not believe that," Alpha seethed. "You knew where they went, and you didn't tell us."

"Please," I pleaded. "Please don't inject me!"

"Weak. Weakness is all I see in your tears," he said coolly. "I had such high hopes for you when you were born. Now, you're a sad, whining, pathetic little boy, and I need to fix that."

43

I shook the table, trying to free myself, jerking as hard as I could at the straps. I howled and pleaded for someone to help me, but no one came to my aid. Alpha jabbed the needle deep into the side of my neck, and the pain exploded as he pushed the plunger down, releasing whatever toxin he had in the syringe into my bloodstream.

"Now show me what kind of soldier you are. Only the strong prevail," he taunted before exiting the room and leaving me to writhe in pain.

The room went dark, and fire erupted through my veins. I screamed until my throat began to crack and bleed from being dry and hoarse. I could taste the blood as it drained down my esophagus, threatening to strangle me. I had experienced these injections so many times that I no longer blacked out from the pain and felt every single nerve ending pop and die as the hellfire surged through my veins. I prayed for death, but to whom I prayed was questionable. To me, there was no god. There was a power-hungry mongrel that called himself God to the humans. But to me, to an angel, an Elohim, a Shining One, I had no god any longer. So, I prayed to death itself, fate, everything that controlled the life and death cycle of angelic beings. The universe, maybe?

I guess I could consider myself lucky that I didn't have to witness Alpha's face billowing in the flames of the Lake of Fire like Luxina did. I had my solitude to endure the pain. I was accustomed to being alone for so long that I felt comfort in the fact I was alone during this, and no one could see my torment to pity me. Pity is one thing I refuse to accept from anyone. Pity shows that you were indeed weak at one point. Pity reflected your character of not being able to overcome struggles. I didn't need pity. I didn't need understanding. I didn't need anything from those who did not empathize with how I felt at that moment. No one was raised solely by Alpha and believed him to be a true father only for him to rear his ugly head and show you how demoralizing he was. Alpha broke whatever love I could feel for parental figures. That's what abuse does to the mind. He had abused me so much that love was most likely impossible for me to experience.

I never could tell how long I lay in writhing pain until it finally subsided. I'm always in a windowless room without a clock, but I'm sure that it was a couple of days this time. Asmodeus came and unbuckled me from the table. I rolled over and vomited up frothy yellow mucus. He scooped me up and carried me to one of the dungeons that had a small window that let light in. He had made up a bed for me against the wall, so I didn't have to lie directly on the floor. Since this was my punishment, he placed one of the shackles on my ankles whether he agreed with it or not. He picked up a ladle from the water bucket and slowly gave me some water to drink. I drank it slowly so I wouldn't choke or immediately heave it back up. The water burned my searing throat at first, but it soon became a soothing, cool rush down my throat. Asmodeus always took care of me after the injections. I don't know what I did to garner his sympathy and empathy, but he was the one person that I never complained to receive it from.

"I'll bring you some food down at dinner time," he assured as he left the room, locking it in place behind him.

"Thank you, Asmodeus," I croaked, barely audibly.

I scooted the bed as close to the window as I could and collapsed into a dreamless sleep. I don't know how long I was asleep before I awoke to a tray being shuffled across the floor with food on it. I walked to the tray near the door and had to lie on my stomach and stretch my arm out to reach it. My fingers grasped the edge of the tray, and I pulled it closer to me. I picked it up and let it sit on my bed. I stared at the tray, wondering if starving myself could gain me a faster death than Alpha's torture. I walked over to the window and punched one of the glass panes out. A cool breeze filled the room, and I closed my eyes, breathing in the scent of the wildflowers growing in the field. The sun was shining brightly while birds chirped and bees buzzed obliviously to my plight. A butterfly happened by, and I reached out of the window for it to land on my hand.

"Queen Mab, if you can hear me, please, save me," I whispered to the butterfly.

It took off from my hand as if to hand-deliver the message personally to the Dark Queen of the Unseelie Court. I walked back over to my bed and scarfed down the food so I wouldn't have to bear the taste of the gruel that was sent for me to eat. Besides, if I wanted to live through these next few weeks, I needed my strength. No sooner had the thought escaped my mind than the doors busted open with the chain gang. Alpha's little gang circled me as if I had anywhere to go. Two tackled me to the floor, with me swinging punches while the other two tossed the chain over the bar in the middle of the floor. They brought the shackles over to my hands and clamped them down over them. They removed the shackle from my foot while two of them hoisted me into the air. Once I was dangling with my feet barely grazing the floor, one of them landed a punch squarely in my ribs. My body absorbed the punch, and my ribs cracked instantly under the pressure.

I gasped in excruciating pain as my lungs struggled harder for air.

"Is that the best you got?" I wheezed, taunting them.

One of them let out a cackling laugh and produced a whip that had an electric charge at the tip. He flicked it once at my body and ripped through my skin with a searing heat. The pain that accompanied the burn was excruciating, however, I never let anyone know if they hurt me. They don't deserve that satisfaction.

"Come on!" I yelled. "More!"

CHAPTER 3

BY THE TIME THEY LEFT the room, the sun had set, and I was a bloody pulp. My wounds oozed and dripped onto the floor below me. I could hardly breathe. Not only had they broken my ribs on one side, but they came in on the other side and cracked them as well, quite possibly puncturing my lung. I could be dead by morning for all I knew. I was to hang like this until Alpha told them to let me down. I was well familiar with the tactic. This time, however, it was more gruesome than all the other times. There was no mercy, and I was never beaten to within inches of life, either.

My nose bled from where they broke it, and I had slash marks all up and down my torso and back from that whip, as well as across my face. The whip was new. They hadn't used it on me before. The door to my cell opened, and Asmodeus rushed in. He untied the chain from the wall and let me down as easily as he could. I definitely couldn't breathe now and shook my head, moaning and choking on air as I gasped. He lifted me back up to the pose I was in and tied the chain back off.

"Boy, I told you to run. You're always thinking of everyone but yourself." He cursed and kicked the water pale that was long empty.

"I couldn't run. I would have led them straight to Xavier and Luxina," I rasped. "Besides, Sophia didn't deserve to die. It was either save her and the twins or run selfishly." I wheezed, and my skin around my ribs sunk deep within as each breath became shallower than the one prior. "I need to tell you something," I began.

"No, don't you dare! I don't need to hear it now. You can tell me tomorrow. You're not dying tonight!" Asmodeus protested.

"I wanted to tell you thank you for your kindness when you don't need to offer any to me," I continued, ignoring him.

"I wasn't always this thing I have become," he said. "I was once a beautiful angel, and I chose to fall with Lilith. I let the darkness consume me. No fault but my own."

"You're still an angel," I croaked. "You may have darkness, but you're still an angel."

He looked up at me with tears threatening to spill. I had never seen him show any type of emotion regarding anyone prior to now.

"Don't you give up," he choked out. "Stay strong. They won't be back tomorrow. They believe you will die tonight. But you show Alpha that no one dictates when you die but you! Incaendiel may not be your father, but you have his will and his fire!"

"How is he?" I inquired through wheezes.

"No one has gone to his cell since he was brought here, and most likely, no one will. Alpha wants to leave him there to rot," Asmodeus scoffed.

"Well, that just won't do," I sniggered.

I sent myself into a violent coughing fit that made it feel as if my ribs burst through my skin.

"That's enough talking for you now," Asmodeus fretted. "I can try to let you down again and get you comfortable in bed."

"No, it will kill me. The blood won't fill my lungs this way. But thank you," I panted.

"I will be back to check on you periodically throughout the night," he said. "Try not to die on me, man. Ok?"

"No promises," I joked.

He frowned, turned on his heels, left the room,

and closed my door behind him. I spent a good portion of the night struggling to breathe and trying not to die. As promised, Asmodeus popped in every so often and offered me small sips of water to keep me hydrated. By morning, the pain was tolerable enough, and my breathing good enough for him to let me down from the chain and then help me over into the bed. As soon as my body touched the bed, the pain shot through me, and I drew in ragged breaths. Asmodeus was dismissed quickly when Lilith entered the room. She carried in her hands the herbs and poultice I had in my room, along with a bowl of water and a washcloth. Asmodeus bowed to her and left without a word. She walked over to my bed and set everything on the floor beside me. She pulled a chair up to the bed, reached down in the water with the washcloth, and wrung it out.

She dabbed the cloth on all my oozing wounds, and I winced as she cleaned them. She worked methodically and had me cleaned up with the salve and herbs applied within minutes. They burned more than usual, but my flesh wounds were deeper than all the times before. I gritted my teeth as she stuffed some of the herbs into deeper wounds. She watched me with curious eyes, but she never spoke a word as she doctored me. By the end of the process, I was drifting off into an exhaustive sleep, praying that I wouldn't have any dreams.

"So, you dream just like the twins?" she asked as she wrapped me in bandages.

"Yes," I managed to croak out.

"What else can you do?" she asked.

I dropped my hand to the floor and searched for the water bowl she had been using to clean me up with. I dipped my finger into the bloody bowl of water, and it instantly froze into a solid block of ice.

"Fire and ice. What a deadly pair," she declared. "That all?" she prodded.

No, I replied with my thoughts.

"Well, well, well," she crooned, lifting an eyebrow. "And I assume Alpha doesn't know?"

"That's right. He knows about the ice but not about the telepathy," I uttered. "Some things are best kept secret."

"So, you were the reason he was able to attack Xavier in his dreams?" she asked.

I nodded. "He hijacked me in my sleep. I received lashings for not telling him about my power."

"Why haven't you run away from him? You have had ample opportunities. Why do you stay?" she countered.

"When I'm not being tortured, I am being controlled by the injections. The moments I have to myself where I am not experiencing either, I have other lives to consider if I were to flee," I maintained. "Not to mention he can track me whether I am cloaked or not."

"How so?" she asked.

"It has to do with the injections. Most likely, a tracker was injected. He told me I would never be able to hide from him."

She leaned in close and whispered in my ear, "We will get you out of here. And when we do, you run, and you don't stop running. You find Luxina and Xavier, and you don't stop looking for whatever can destroy him until you have found it. Understand me?" she stipulated.

I nodded. "Yes, ma'am," I conceded.

"Now you hush up with that ma'am crap. Call me Grandmother if you wish. I am your grandmother as much as I am the twins' grandmother," she responded with a smile and wink.

"Yes, Grandmother," I answered with a hint of a smile.

I felt comforted around her. A warmth radiated from her that I never experienced with Alpha. All you felt around him was a cold despair that wrought you to your bones. She stood to leave when I caught her hand. Is this what unconditional love feels like? A love that you didn't have to fight to win the affection of? A love that came with no strings attached, no fulfillments to be made. Pure, unadulterated love?

"Will you stay?" I begged. "Until I fall asleep?"

She smiled at me and squeezed my hand. "I thought you would never ask," she cooed.

By the time I had awakened, she was gone, and the sunlight poured through the window. I struggled to sit up in bed. My body was a mess. Aches and pains popped up in places I didn't even remember being hit. My ribs screamed in resistance, and my lungs ached for deep breaths of air, but I managed to sit straight up in the bed. I moved my feet off the side of the bed and tested the strength of my legs. They were still wobbly, but I could stand without hitting the ground. I hobbled over to the window of my cell and looked out as dark clouds began to cover the sky. I could smell the rain in the air as it drifted into the window.

Tiny droplets began to fall, splattering my face as they hit the concrete slabs of the tiny window. I crouched to the floor beside the window and just watched as the storm brewed. Lightning crashed, and thunder rolled as the rain fell harder. The harder it rained, the darker my mood became. Or was it vice versa? Did I wake up in darkness? Did it matter? Gale force winds tore through the tiny meadow beside my window. Much to my astonishment, the rain turned to ice and snow, and within minutes, snow began to pile up outside of the tiny window. Ice began to form around me in my cell, and I watched it crawl its way up the walls, freezing every inch of the cell into solid ice.

Everything, except me.

A pounding came to the door.

"Damian! Damian, you must stop!" Lilith yelled through the frozen door.

I ignored her as the storm outside grew heavier and the winds picked up to hurricane force levels. It was at that moment that my own questions were answered. It was me.

"Damian! You're going to kill us all!" she pleaded through the door.

What do I care if everyone dies? Everyone that was here was now on Alpha's side. There was no chance for me, for Xavier, or for Luxina to live through this hell. Maybe it would be better this way. I am no longer a threat to anyone. No one is a threat anymore. The world is saved.

"The world is not saved! Alpha isn't susceptible to this power of yours. You're killing everyone but him. You're just doing him a favor and taking lives and spilling blood that should be on his hands and not yours. Please, you must stop!"

I couldn't stop it. They all deserved to pay, even if it didn't affect Alpha. I could take him out easier without his minions around.

"Damian! Incaendiel is here. Luxina will never forgive you if you kill him! He is innocent in all this! He has been the one trying to defeat him from the beginning. You kill him, and you kill whatever chance this world must be saved."

That was the only thing that could stop me. She was right there. I couldn't kill Incaendiel. I couldn't take him away from Luxina. I looked out the window, and the snow began to pitter out. The dark clouds began to move away, and the sun slowly came back out, shining as brightly as it had been earlier. The ice began to melt from the walls, and the water pooled around my feet. The door to my cell swung open, and I expected the chain gang back in here to chain me up once more for my little temper tantrum. Instead, it was just Lilith who stood there.

"They won't be back," she assured. "May I come in?"

"Oh, there's a choice now?" I retaliated.

"Fair enough," she answered, walking in. "So, what was all that?"

I shrugged my shoulders. "I didn't even know I was doing it until you came along."

"Alpha has no idea it was you who froze hell over," she mused, sitting down in the chair beside my bed. "And I plan to keep it that way."

"He must know it was me. It's not the first time I have used my powers," I corrected.

"Yes, he has seen ice come from your hand and be directed at a target. However, the ice crept up and covered everything, unlike your normal ice blasts," she proclaimed, pursing her lips and knitting her eyebrows together. "We need to keep it that way, too. No more freak ice takeovers, no matter how much you hate us all."

"I don't hate you all," I retorted. "I'm just tired… I'm tired of this twilight I am stuck in. Half between heaven and half between hell… the darkness that comes in waves... the loneliness and isolation. I don't want to do this anymore. I can't do this anymore. Always fearful that I will be beaten and tortured. Afraid that one more injection is all it would take for me to be a puppet forever to Alpha. Afraid that one more injection and I could kill the two people I care most about than myself. That's what he is going to have me do. In the end days, I will be the one forced to kill Luxina and Xavier."

"When the next opportunity comes up, you must run. Don't think of anyone you are leaving behind. Don't worry about the deaths that will come at the cost of your escape. You must GO!" she pleaded.

"And what then? Be hunted down by mutts? Lead them straight to the people I want to protect," I snapped. "Every way this scenario goes, I lead him to the very people that need to be as far away from him as possible."

"You're going to have to take that chance. If they do follow you, Xavier is trained to fight them off by your side. Fight and don't stop fighting. Even in the end, when all hope seems lost, don't stop fighting!"

"I don't know if I can promise that," I whimpered in choked words as tears threatened the backs of my eyes.

"Don't promise. Just when the time comes, and you will know what that time is in that very moment, you fight!" she repeated.

I nodded, accepting her words. She stood from her seat and walked to the door. "I don't know when or how long it will take, but we will get you out of here." With those last words, she left the room and shut the door behind her.

CHAPTER 4

THE SEASONS CAME and went as I sat in the dungeon I was cursed into. I had lost count of the days once the beatings had begun again. I had just recovered from the broken ribs when Alpha sent the chain gang back in. I guess Lilith could only have so much say in what happened to me while I was here in Alpha's clutches. I never did get broken ribs again, though. I did, however, receive the sharp end of the whip countless times. Whoever created that whip was first on my kill list when I busted out of this prison cell. My body was littered with scars from the bites it left with each strike. They hardly ever fed me. Asmodeus would sneak me food whenever he could, but even that was sparse. If this was Alpha's idea of breaking me, he had no idea what it would take to break me into a conformed soldier completely.

One thing I was allowed to do in between the beatings was read. I asked Lilith to bring me the books from my room down to the dungeon as well as grab me new ones from the library wing. She was the only person I allowed in the room to see me. I had not seen Sophie since the last day in my room, although Lilith had told me many times that she wished to see me. I never acknowledged the thought, so she never stopped by. The last I saw Lucifer was when he told me to kill Sophia. That I will never get over. Sophia was his soulmate, his one true half. His black heart held no bounds regarding the women in his life. He was as much of a monster as Alpha was.

I picked up the books lying around my bed and thumbed through the pages I had memorized. I had read through every book of mythology I could get my hands on. There had to be an inkling of research on what it meant to be a Shining One. I would scan through the pages and set the book aside, picking up another to take its place. Nothing. I could never find anything. I tossed the books to the floor in frustration as I balled myself up on the bed, tucking my arms deep under my armpits. In these moments of solitude, it wasn't hard for my thoughts to drift to Luxina and Xavier and wonder how they were faring, staying safe from the hunting parties Alpha executed. In truth, those two were the only things keeping me going at this point.

I sighed heavily and looked at the window that was now boarded up. Alpha had them board it up today as if taking away my one piece of time mattered. I still had my memories of sunshine, of wilderness, of rainstorms. He could take away the view, but he couldn't board up my mind. I hadn't seen anyone all day long and hoped that it meant there wouldn't be any torture for the day. Just a moment of respite is all I needed. My eyes were heavy, and I had staved off sleep for so many days, fearing the moment they closed, I would be strung up once more to endure the whip. I closed my eyes and drifted off to sleep for the first time in days.

Harrowing images flooded my mind. I watched as Alpha rode through the sky in the chariot he had used to fly to Stygia. It was being pulled along by the same horses as before. A red one, a black one, a white one, and a pale gray one. Something tugged at my mind from scripture. It dawned on me what the significance of those four horses meant. They were the horses of the apocalypse. War, famine, pestilence, and death. Below him in the valley, hordes of creatures crept, slithered, crawled, and bounded in one massive black wave toward the angel fleet that was stationed on the corresponding side of the valley. Fire and brimstone rained from the sky, exploding as they hit the ground below. Those standing in the wake of destruction burned to crisps, leaving an ashen body, or were struck down into pillars of salt that blew away in the wind.

The advancing mass of creatures had draugrs, werewolves, vampires, demons both greater and lower, and whatever other mutts Alpha had created in his laboratory using stolen Seelie blood. I watched, waiting for Lilith or Lucifer to appear at his side, but neither of the two was there. Sophie was nowhere to be seen as well. However, Incaendiel stood at the forefront of the army of angels who all stood waiting for his command to charge against the stampede hurtling toward them. The ground broke free beneath the angel army and flames tore through the sky as they all fell to a burning grave.

I tried to move, but I stood waist deep in a tarry, black pit that I struggled to free myself from. I looked to my right and left, and stuck alongside myself I found Luxina and Xavier struggling to free themselves as well from the hot, oily substance. No matter how much we struggled, we just sank deeper without breaking free. Alpha arrived at the pit with a laugh.

"Join me and be free," he yelled, laughing maniacally.

"Never!" I seethed.

"Then die, young Shining Ones." Alpha stared at us emotionlessly. His eyes were like bottomless pits, cavernous and oblique. It was a look I had never witnessed before in his cold, dead-set eyes. He had completely gone off the deep end and most likely had planned something even more terrifying than the nature of the apocalypse. I heard the sound of a gong and a loud crack in the air. I watched in frozen horror as molten lava came racing toward us across the valley, burning all the creatures he had made. From behind us, water crashed through the valley. The universe seemed to implode on itself as bits and pieces of planets and asteroids rained down around us, along with the fire and brimstone. Every star in the sky seemed to supernova and explode all at once, and just as he had sparked the universe into existence, he began to dismantle it.

New beings swarmed the air. They had the wings of angels and the grotesque, disfigured faces of animals. No doubt, these were more of Alpha's experiments. When they opened their eyes, they shone like the sun. He had done it. He had created his muddled shining ones that were half demon, half shining one.

"If I can't have what rightfully belongs to me, no one will," Alpha bellowed. "I will just start over and do it the right way." It was then that the lava and waters reached Luxina, Xavier, and me in the pit just as we reached for each other's hands.

I woke from the dream, choking and gasping, fighting the air around me with all my might. My senses finally came to me as my surroundings materialized around me. I was safely tucked away in the dungeon. Well, as safe as safe can be compared to that nightmare I just had. I sat up on the side of my bed and ran my hands through my sweat-riddled hair. Was that just a nightmare? Or was that something more? Is that what the end will look like? I stood up and began to anxiously pace the floor.

A gentle breeze filled my room, and I looked at the door to see if someone had entered it while I was lost in deep thought. No one had opened it, and the window couldn't let enough air into the room to cause that building wind in the room. Papers I had been writing on began to blow around the room as well as the books I had tossed casually to the floor earlier. I held my hand up to my face to protect it from anything that might strike me from the whirlwind forming in the room. A translucent, window-type thing appeared before me, and a little old woman stepped in from the most marvelous oasis you could imagine.

"Hello, Damian," she greeted. "I'm Starfire." The hole she stepped through stayed up behind her as the winds ripped around the room. "Come with me, child. I can keep you safer than Lilith can."

"Who are you?" I marveled incredulously. "How do you know who I am?"

"I'm the Oracle, and time is running out. Your dream was much more than just a dream. You got a taste of what the end of days looks like for every being that exists in this universe," she postulated.

"How do you know that?" I refuted. "How do I know this isn't some trick?"

"I told you. I am the Oracle. I have seen what

you have seen, and I am the only one who can give you and your siblings what you need to defeat Alpha. Come with me," she repeated, extending her hand.

"Are they there? Luxina and Xavier?" I stammered. "Are they safe?"

"They are close, but they are not here yet," she replied. "They will arrive safely in due time, but you, I am afraid if you don't escape soon, there will be no end of days for you to see." Her face was grave as she spoke the words to me. "Please, take my hand and come with me."

I shook my head. "I can't. I must save Incaendiel first."

"You have to stop trying to save everyone before there's no one left to save," she rebutted.

Why does everyone keep telling me that? It is so frustrating to hear it over and over.

"Once he is safely away from Alpha, I will come to you," I promised. "I will make it!"

She frowned and shook her head. "You, my child, have a heart bigger than the universe. I will see you soon."

She turned to walk back through the slice of world that floated in the room.

"Wait!" I yelled.

She turned around with a look of hope on her face that I may have changed my mind.

"If I don't make it, if I don't get to see them again, tell them I did everything I could to keep them safe. And I'm sorry. I am so deeply sorry."

"Tell them yourself," she replied with a smile, stepping through the translucent hole.

It disappeared from my room, and the wind died down, dropping everything to the ground it had been tossing about. One of the books dropped open, and I picked it up to close it when the title header caught my attention.

꒭ꟼꝆꝫꝆꝫꝪꝆꟼꝆꝆꝫ꒭

I HAD STUDIED every ancient language, and this was the original language of them all. The title was in Enochian, my own language. The angelic alphabet wrapped its letters across the pages of the book I held. I couldn't help but smile, knowing that this was a gift from the Oracle who had just left. I poured over the pages, reading as much as it offered about what I was.

The Shining Ones were an old race of Elder Gods who died out prior to the big spark of the universe referred to as the big bang. They were a superior race who had powers beyond any god or goddess that existed within the realm. They had faces that shone as bright as the sun, eyes that glowed like burning stars, and they glowed like a raging wildfire from their own internal flames that burned through their bodies. Their wings were as bright as gold, and their skin as white as snow. They always came in pairs as twin flames.

The prophecy foretold of a special birth of three that would wield powers of both fire and ice to rule the universe as one. Any and all lower gods that stood in their way would be made to bow to their powerful majesty. The three special Shining Ones who were to be birthed would be unstoppable as a trio but would ultimately bring the balance of the universe together after many failed attempts of power-hungry gods. With the birthing of the special trio, they were given powers as a pair. The one that wields fire and the one that wields ice would be the rulers of the new world order as part of the new God and Goddess quartet. The third Shining One would ultimately be absorbed by the twin since they were never meant to be three of them in the end.

Humanity has all but wiped out the very notion and idea of the Shining Ones after church rose to power through the manipulations of the god they worship as the one true god. While the church holds its grasp over the world, so does the lower god who helped create it.

The Shining Ones were called by many names, such

as the Anunnaki, Elohim, and even angels. However, the names do not give these carefully crafted beings the justice they deserve. Angels were created by gods and goddesses and do not contain the power of their masters. However, Shining Ones are above the class of gods and goddesses, and to be rudimentarily referred to as an angel is an error. These great beings comprised the original seven members of the Council of El prior to their dying off.

I closed the book, and it vanished into thin air. It was only for my eyes, it seemed. The words of Starfire echoed in my mind, of her urgent pleas for me to join up with Xavier and Luxina. The three of us together was the only way to stop Alpha. She was right. But there were so many things that were left out. How could the twin flames not be meant to be with one another? Xavier and Luxina were supposed to be together, not Luxina and me. Did that mean that Sophie and Incaendiel were never the true god and goddess to be? Just the ones responsible for the creation of the new world order? And what was the whole absorbed thing? Is Xavier truly not meant to exist?

Thousands of questions rolled through my head as I processed the information overload. There would absolutely be no way Luxina or I would absorb Xavier. So, what then? Is that why the world ends in the apocalyptic dream? Because we are still all together, and it isn't just Luxina and me? The realization of my thoughts sank deeply in, and that's when I knew for a fact that we were all doomed. There was no way we could defeat Alpha without this key fact.

The door opened, and Alpha's chain gang walked in. I groaned inwardly and shut my eyes, waiting for them to tackle me to the ground. I slowly opened my eyes and noticed they had just congregated around the door. They didn't come bearing chains, either.

"Alpha wishes to see you," Mammon stated, swinging the door wider for me to follow them.

I walked over to them, and two led in front of me with two behind me as we climbed the stairs from the dungeon. I walked the familiar halls with a mind heavy with knowledge. The fate of the universe, the fate of myself and siblings, all of it swirled around in my head. We passed by the doors that had been barricaded, and bricks now stood mortared in place as the screams of the beasts within the walls echoed through the hall. It was always hard to drown those sounds out of my head. At times, they haunted my dreams as well as haunting my every waking thought.

They led me down the all too familiar hallway to the door behind which Alpha sat at his desk. The door opened, and the two who stood in front of me parted ways. I walked alone into the room. Alpha had his usual demeanor he donned while quietly studying me as I walked to a chair and took a seat. There was a long moment of silence between us. I could only assume he was trying to think of the right words to say or the right question to ask. I stared back at him unblinking, hoping that my poker face was as believable as it had always been.

"You look terrible," he finally spoke.

"I suppose I do," I remarked. "I'm sure you already knew of what my condition was prior to bringing me here."

He smiled a sinister grin. "You are quite right, my boy. You are quite right."

He tapped his forefingers together as he contemplated his next words to speak to me.

"I have a small task for you," he said, leaning back in his chair and resting his feet up on the desk.

"And what would that be?" I asked.

"I want you to be the one to speak to Incaendiel. Get whatever information you can out of him. He hasn't been seen nor touched the entire time he has been here and locked away just as you were. It's time someone goes in to try and break him." Alpha replied.

"What makes you think he would talk to me?" I asked. "He most likely hates me. I know he despises Lucifer and equally despises you. I'm your pawn in all this. What makes you think he would tell me anything?"

"Because there's more to the way Incaendiel works than just being fueled by hatred or rage. He is methodical. The ringleader of all. He says jump, the others ask how high. He is superior to them all, and they acknowledge that. Everyone except you, that is. I believe he would talk to you," he replied earnestly.

"What? You want me to go now?" I asked.

"Yes," Alpha replied, a bit agitated. He composed his face and, with a smile, said, "The sooner, the better."

He was trying to sweet talk me into doing his dirty work is what all this was. I nodded and stood from the chair.

"And Damian," he started.

"Yes, sir?" I asked, stepping to the door and opening it.

"Don't fail this time," he stated venomously.

"I don't know what to base pass and fail with you anymore. So, I will try, sir, to not fail you," I retorted, closing the door behind me.

Alpha's escorts waited for me outside of his doors, ready to rush in at a moment's notice. I saw the tension ease from their shoulders as I walked out of the door, closing it behind me.

"Take me to Incaendiel," I ordered.

They looked at one another hesitantly.

"Do you really want me to open that door again and have him tell you?" I asked, aggravated.

They exchanged glances and led me from Alpha's door back down toward the dungeons.

CHAPTER 5

"BEFORE YOU GO IN, Damian, there is something we would like to say," Mammon began. "We didn't sign up for this. Alpha assigned us this detail. And you know the punishment for disobeying his orders. You say the word, and you won't have to stay to suffer anymore."

"Why does everyone want to help me escape?" I asked, shaking my head.

"Because you will become our new leader one day," Mammon replied.

He slipped a blade in my hand. I looked down at the gift and then back up to meet his eyes. I nodded my head, slipped the blade into my pocket, and pushed the door open to Incaendiel's dungeon. It was dark in the room, with hardly a sliver of light coming from the boarded-up window across from where he was chained. I flipped the light switch on in the room, and he squinted through the blinding light. Recognition registered on his face, and a glare replaced the once confused look. He looked at the door, I suppose waiting for more people to follow me in. When I walked closer into the light, his look of anger faded away to pity. It was then the questions started pouring from his mind. *Were they feeding him? Were they torturing him?* He took notice of the scar on my neck the whip had left behind. A moment of insecurity struck me, and I didn't want to do this. I didn't want to report anything to Alpha that was said. But I had to report something. I squared my shoulders and walked over to Incaendiel. I pulled up a chair and sat down, staring at him, his stare equally matching mine. And then his thoughts changed. *I wonder what Alpha wants him to do to me?*

"Nothing," I replied.

I watched as he processed what I had just done. His face went from surprise to confusion and then to downright bafflement. I tried to act casually and leaned my chair back lifting the legs off the floor and looped my arms behind my head. It was kind of fun playing cat and mouse.

"I know. It's confusing. And no, Alpha has no idea," I replied with a confident grin.

I watched the realization hit him. "You can read minds?" he asked, a bit unbelieving.

"Yes, but I haven't always been able to. I'm sure it is something that has to do with the experiments that Alpha does on me," I replied with a shrug. "It may have been the connection with my siblings that triggered it. I will never know. All I know is that one day, I could hear the thoughts of every person who stood in the room with me. Some may think it's a curse, some a blessing. I find it to be a useful asset in times of war."

"Your mother and I could read each other's minds. It might have something to do with that," he offered.

"She is not my mother," I replied heatedly.

I tried to compose myself.

"Why do you say that, Damian? Why do you speak of Sophie in such ill regard?" he asked.

I hated it whenever anyone mentioned Sophie being my mother. I looked at his face as he read me. He had no idea that Sophie was even alive or that she had turned out to be on Alpha's side. He had no idea what he was protecting from Alpha she was trying to fork over. I couldn't tell him that. I couldn't be the one to break that news.

"She may have created me with my father, but neither of them will ever be my parents. They will never understand me. They will never understand the endured torture I have been put through while being with Alpha."

He nodded in understanding.

"You know, Luxina and you have that temper thing going for yourselves. She gets angered and explodes into fire so easily. I can't imagine who she gets that from," he said with a chuckle.

"From my understanding, she gets it from you," I replied with a smirk.

"What does he want with me, Damian?" he asked.

"The same thing he wanted with me. The same thing he wanted with Sophie, and the same thing he wanted with my brother and sister," I replied. "He wants to build an army of new angels."

"I thought he no longer had the power to create? He can't just go around injecting people, hoping the injections take. And I certainly hope he doesn't think we can procreate a new race for him," he said, still not knowing everything that I do.

"He isn't going to do any of that," I replied with a sincere, concerned look.

"What are his plans?" he asked.

I looked around the room and leaned forward to him, the chair legs settling softly on the floor. "Once our blood accepts these injections, he plans to use Lilith at his side to create a special race from our newly formed blood. The creations won't be mindless anymore because he has Lilith at his side now. However, they thought the original werewolves and vampires were horrible in the beginning, but these new creatures, these new angels he wants to make... they will destroy everything." I stared at him with bewilderment and fear.

"Why are you helping him?" he asked. "Why do you fear this plan but still help him?"

"I have no choice," I replied, straightening up and returning to my position in the chair I had been in. The nonchalant, not caring attitude washed back over me, and I had to play it cool once more.

"We all have a choice, Damian," he replied. "There has to be a reason you are helping him."

"Who says I am truly helping him?" I replied with a sly grin.

"You helped him take Luxina and Xavier," he stammered in confusion.

"Incorrect. Lucifer was the one that orchestrated both of those incidents, not I," I replied. "I don't want them anywhere near Alpha."

"Afraid he would choose them over you, and you would be the outcast once more?" he asked, a bit too sarcastic. I appreciated his wit more than he could understand.

"Yes," I replied very quietly and simply. "And

they don't deserve that as a punishment."

I watched as he processed everything I had said. He was beginning to realize that I truly wasn't just some soldier for Alpha that was manipulated my entire life. He was seeing me for me.

"You care for them, don't you?" he asked, squinting at me suspiciously.

"Why wouldn't I? They are what I am missing in life. They are my blood," I replied. "I keep everyone at arm's length. I don't wish to get close to anyone. It's been my thing since I was a youngster. Alpha never showed me what love is. He never showered me with affection. He just wanted me to create this stupid army of his. However, I have seen the way Luxina looks at me. She looks at me with love, empathy, and sorrow. She doesn't see me as a monster. At least, she didn't until the attack of the Watchers. I have no idea what her thoughts of me are at this moment. She could hate me for all I care. All that matters is that she and Xavier stay safe and as far away from Alpha as I can keep them."

"So, when you took her from me, all those things you said. Your cold demeanor... that wasn't you?" he asked.

I shook my head. "The injections Alpha gives me make me vulnerable to mind control. I must do whatever I am told. Lucifer struck a deal with Alpha to deliver both Xavier and Luxina to him in exchange for me. Alpha took the deal, but he won't hold up his end of the bargain even if he still had them in his grasp. Alpha needs us."

"Mother created us. She can create more of us. Why does he need us in specific?" he asked.

"Because the Unseelie Queen will no longer help him, nor will she aid Lilith in creating more of the Shining Ones. I also don't foresee Lilith remaining in the end," I replied, shifting in my seat. "She is the key to it all…" I was about to tell him everything I knew. He needed to know from beginning to end what was going to happen. To hell with Alpha. He could return me to the dungeon if he wished to. This was what was important.

"How?" he began when the door busted open.

Lucifer walked in, grinning from ear to ear. "Ah, son, starting early, are we?" he asked, walking over to me. "Did Alpha give the orders to start on him?"

"Yes and no," I replied, settling my chair back on the ground and standing up. Why was he always ruining things? "We were just having a small chat. I needed to know where my siblings might be hiding and who, but their father would know that answer. However, you interrupted."

I reached out to Incaendiel with my thoughts. *I will return to speak with you again. I have a lot to fill you in on before things get so out of hand that they cannot be controlled. There will be another visitor, and after they leave, I will be back to free you.* He looked at me and nodded with his eyes, acknowledging what I had told him through telepathy.

"Well, does he know where they are? Do we need to force it out of him?" Lucifer asked, grinning madly.

"He doesn't know," I replied, walking to the door.

"And you believe him?" Lucifer shouted.

I spun on my heels and pinned Lucifer against the wall. I wanted to take him out right then and there, but I knew I wouldn't be able to make it safely from this place if I did. "Do you question my authority?" I demanded, glaring at Lucifer. "He doesn't know."

I could see the fear settling on Lucifer's face, and it was most satisfying. I hoped he could feel the hatred I had for him leach from within me and flow through his body.

"That is not how you talk to me! I am your superior, and I am your father! You will respect me!" Lucifer bellowed.

"Respect is earned, and you do not have a single respectable bone in your pathetic existence," I retorted.

"Is that why you're in here? Buttering up to Incaendiel in hopes he would adopt you as his?" Lucifer demanded.

"At least he proves to be a better father than you ever have," I seethed. "Now, leave the room and do not bother the prisoner. Alpha wants him to remain untouched and unharmed. Those are orders!"

I stomped from the room with Lucifer hot on my trail. No one met me on the other side of the door to lead me anywhere. I pushed forward as fast as I could to get away from Lucifer before I sank a dagger into his heart.

"I'm not done talking to you!" he yelled down the hall, his voice echoing and bouncing off the walls.

I turned on my heel and faced him, clenching my fists and calming myself before he knew about my power.

"What do you want?" I demanded through clenched teeth.

"You need to change your attitude toward me and toward your mother!" he roared, pointing his finger and jabbing it in my chest.

I grabbed his hand and twisted the finger that jabbed me until I felt it cave and break under my grip. I pushed him with his broken hand against the adjacent wall from us and gripped it even tighter.

"You listen to me!" I yelled. "You will NEVER be my father. She will NEVER be my mother. You brought my brother and sister here for Alpha to do to them what I have been subjected to for years. I do not hate them. You may hate those two, but they are innocent in all this, and I will not stand by and watch you and everyone else wreck what I have left in this world on a power trip! My advice to you is to stay away from me because next time, I won't hesitate to drive a blade so deep in your chest that no one could pry it from your lifeless body."

As the words left my mouth, I pulled the blade I had been given and threw it to the ground. He watched with fearful eyes, not knowing where I had gotten the blade.

"You are not my superior. You're just another pawn in Alpha's chess game. And the next time you interrupt me when I am doing what I was told to do, I will no doubt kill you for insubordination."

I released the grip I had on his now crushed hand and continued my way up from the dungeon and headed to Alpha's office. I opened the door without even knocking, and Sophie and Lilith were sitting around his desk. They all turned to look at me, surprised to see me in the office.

"I was unable to perform my job," I stated curtly to Alpha. "Lucifer interrupted me while I was speaking with the prisoner and turned everything personal. I will have to go a second time to get whatever information you need."

Alpha motioned me in the room, and I closed the door behind me.

"What did Lucifer do to stop your interrogation?" Alpha asked.

"He busted in and asked me if I was there on

your orders to interrogate the prisoner, to which I replied yes. He then began to badger the prisoner, interrupting even further. When that wasn't enough for him, he began to drag personal history between the two of us into the interrogation. You can find him down near the dungeons with a crushed hand after he threatened me. I told him his next act of subordination when speaking to his superior would be death."

I relayed everything in my soldier attitude that I had always shouldered.

"I have my boy back," Alpha replied, grinning. "Instruct Mammon to take Lucifer to the dungeons and string him up for his insubordination."

"Yes, sir," I replied with almost a click of my heels.

I began to leave the room when Alpha stopped me.

"And Damian?" he began.

"Yes, sir?" I asked.

"Sleep in your room tonight," he replied as he glanced through papers that were on his desk.

I could only get a brief glance at them before I was formally dismissed from the room. It looked like some sort of mechanism he was building. It almost looked like an iron heart.

As I left the room, Sophie followed behind me.

"Why did you do that?" she asked angrily.

"Lucifer just wants to talk to you."

"When will you all get it through your thick skulls that I do not care about any of you, or what will happen to you?" I replied vehemently.

"We just want what's best for you," she replied, trying to tuck a lock of my hair behind my ear.

I swatted her hand away.

"NO, you just want what's best for yourselves. And at what expense? Incaendiel is locked in the dungeon and has been locked away for as long as I have been locked away. You're trying to hand my brother and sister over to the very man that turned me into some kind of killing machine. You are the monster in this scenario. You don't see how well you are playing into Alpha's hand. You never will."

"Incaendiel is here?" she asked, bewildered.

"Oh, your master and mother didn't tell you? See the secrets they don't even tell you? What side are you truly on because obviously, to them, you are not on their side. That makes you expendable. If I were you, I would watch my back. I was sentenced away for not fulfilling a fool's plan. What do you think you would have to do to be locked away and tortured as I was?"

"Which cell is his?" she asked.

I rolled my eyes. "As if you care."

"I do!" she hissed.

"He's in the very last cell in the bottom of the dungeon," I replied. "But don't tell him I sent you."

She nodded and whisked away down the steps. I headed to my room and slammed the door shut. All this drama was getting on my nerves. Why did the angelic realm have to be full of so much malice and hatred when it was supposed to be the epitome of unconditional love?

A quiet knock came on my door, and I opened it, expecting some other person to cause me more agitation. Asmodeus stood there with a plate of food and some water.

"Alpha sent this for you," he said as he walked into my room and set my food down on the tabletop.

I quickly glanced up and down the hall before shutting the door behind him.

"It's good to see you out of that dungeon. You don't deserve that treatment," Asmodeus raved as he wrapped me in a hug.

"We don't have much time before spying ears and eyes come along. I have a plan that I need your help with," I stated hurriedly.

"What is it?" he asked, sitting down in the chair at the table.

"I'm going to break Incaendiel out and leave with him, and I need your help to do it."

He mulled over the idea before speaking. "What do you need me to do?" he asked.

"Incaendiel is expecting a visitor from me to

signal him that it's time. You're to untie his chains so he is at full power," I explained. "We will then fight our way out or die trying."

"That plan has so many flaws in it," Asmodeus replied, shaking his head.

"Please, you are the only person that can help pull this off. Everyone wants me to escape, but I also need Incaendiel to get to safety as well. Please, Asmodeus, help me."

"I will see what I can do. I am sure others here will help you as well. There have been building murmurs within the ranks about how Alpha has been treating you poorly when you have done everything you can for him. There will be riots soon if he hurts you more than what he has," Asmodeus stated.

"Will you come with us? When we escape?" I asked.

"We will see when the time comes," Asmodeus said with an appreciative smile. "Your safety first."

"Do you know what Alpha plans to do with me now?" I asked.

"We haven't heard anything lately. But rumor has it that he has been building the gladiator rink up with new, ferocious beasts," he replied grimly.

"I see," I said. I couldn't stop the defeat from pouring through me.

"You will survive it. You always do," he replied, patting me on my back. "Eat up. You will need your strength."

He left the room, and I sank into the chair he had just been sitting in. This would be my final trial. My final test. This was my life-or-death moment. Once I walked into that gladiator ring, it was either kill or be killed. I have fought werewolves, vampires, and every other concoction Alpha has thrown my way and came out a victor on the other side. This time, however, I was disadvantaged. I was skin and bones. I hadn't trained in nearly a year. I had been beaten and starved almost to the point of death so many times I had lost count of the brushes of death I had.

I stared at the food that was left for me on the table with crippling nausea. I didn't know how long I had before I was tossed into that ring, and right now, I couldn't stomach food. Maybe I could escape before the time came. I knew it wouldn't be possible, though. I had just been granted freedom from the dungeon. I couldn't do anything without being caught in the act.

I picked at the food on my plate and just pushed it away. If it was my time for death, then it would be my time. I would give it my all and fight to the end. If fate had different plans for me, then so be it.

CHAPTER 6

THEY CAME FOR ME at night in the grips of one of the apocalyptic nightmares that riddled my every moment of sleep. I awoke thrashing and kicking, trying to escape the nightmare I had been in.

Damian…

Damian!

"Damian!" the voice called, breaking me from the nightmare.

I glanced around the room, trying to clear my head and understand what was going on. Asmodeus, Mammon, and a few others stood around my bed, each holding something in their hand. Asmodeus held out the gladiator outfit for me to change into. Mammon held the scissors to cut my hair. I stripped in front of them and donned the ridiculous outfits I was forced to wear whenever I fought in these stupid games that Alpha held. Mammon walked up behind me and began to cut all my red, curly locks away until I was nearly bald. The others held out weapons for me to fasten. I had a mace, an axe, a long sword, a short sword, dueling knives, and a bow and arrow quiver. I strapped each of the special weapons all over my body. These weren't your average weapons. They were the size of an ink pen, and when you clicked a button on the side, they transformed into the weapon at hand. Everything, that is, but the bow and quiver of arrows. They then oiled down my bare skin so I would be less susceptible to scratches.

"Are you ready?" Asmodeus asked.

I cocked an eyebrow at him. I most likely looked like death. It had been several weeks since Alpha had allowed me back into my room, and I was just starting to be able to eat and keep food down.

"As ready as I can be," I replied.

He nodded and stepped aside. Two of them led me in front, with two on my sides and two flanking me in case I tried to run. That chance was long past. Asmodeus had begged me every night to flee, but I couldn't. My conscience wouldn't let me leave here without at least trying to break Incaendiel free. I had to do it for Luxina. I was told I was too noble for my own good. That may be it: pride. But I sure as hell was going to try and do what was right. Had I known I would have been subjected to the torture I had endured, I wouldn't have even brought him back. I didn't get a pat on the head or anything for obeying orders.

The gladiator ring was more or less a colossal stadium that Alpha had erected. Those that attended it either loved it or hated it. They loved the death, the chaos, and the gore. Some loved to watch me fight to the death with all these creatures, screaming in the crowd with joy as they got to watch the battles. Others sat quietly, less than enthused by the show. They abhorred the idea that Alpha would go to the lengths that he did for a little entertainment for those in the compound. I was led to the iron gate where I was placed, a gate closing behind me to lock me inside and make sure I didn't try to flee. I would stand there until the gate rose and let me into the arena where I had to ready myself within seconds before they opened the other doors for the mountains of creatures to attack.

I stood silently, readying my weapons on my side, and the gate slid shut behind me. I turned to see the group that had led me to the death rink staring at me with grief, awe, and a mix of emotions.

"See you all on the other side," I smirked.

I could already hear the cheers and jeers from the crowd awaiting the release of the gates. I scanned the crowd through the holes of the gate to see who all sat in the crowd. I saw Alpha on his throne at the center, with Lilith and Sophie on either side of him. Of course, they would be here. I heard the gears creak as the chain began to move, working the gate up so that I could enter the stadium. A hush fell over the crowd as I stepped forward into what was most likely the last place I would ever see.

Normally, there were loud voices yelling out in the air when I came into this place. But not this time. Every person there remained quiet, almost as if it were a protest. I pulled a sword from my side and clicked the activating button. The long sword materialized in my hand, and I readied myself for the onslaught of whatever Alpha had made special for this evening. A rumble came to the ground as they raised all the gates at once. I wasn't prepared for that. Normally, it's one at a time until I have killed them all. Panic flew through me as my eyes swept gate to gate, wondering what to expect first.

The first creature to emerge was directly to my left, and I could smell its breath before I could even see it walk out from the darkened tunnel. A putrid smell filled the arena, mixed with a nauseating gaseous smell, almost like the smell of death in a bottle. I turned my attention to the tunnel, waiting for it to come out into the light. I questioned whether I really would make it out of this fight as soon as it walked from the darkness and out for me to see. It had the body of a werewolf, but this one was much different than the ones I had been used to fighting. It was twice the size of the ones Alpha had been producing for me to fight. Green beady eyes stared me down as it sniffed the air. Drool dropped from its jaws and sizzled as it hit the ground. Most likely, he had altered the saliva to pure acid. Would it eat through my weapons?

I had no time to sit and wonder what would happen as the beast leapt toward me, its muzzle snapping and snarling as it cleared twenty feet in a single bound. The thing was huge, and muscles rippled throughout its body. Patches of fur fell off with each movement of its body, exposing the sickly green color of its skin. Its tail was like that of a lizard and upon closer inspection, its clawed paws were more like hands. I scrambled back as it bounded within inches of my face, swiping with my sword. I tripped and fell to my back, barrel rolling into a crouch. I had cut through the skin right under the eye, and it immediately healed.

"What the—" I muttered as it didn't waste a moment countering my attack with a swipe of its own clawed fingers.

I rolled again out of the way as I saw another one

of the beasts emerge from the gate. It spotted me and came careening directly for me. One thing was for sure: they were hungry and most likely hadn't eaten for weeks. I thought back to the hallway I had been led through up to Alpha, where the walls had been sealed with bricks and mortar. The howls that came from the other side… it was most likely these things.

I had to get my head in the zone. Both of those things were closing in on me. I clicked another sword to life from my side and began to fight the one closest to me. Its claws parried the blows almost as if they were made of metal themselves. I swiped with one sword while distracting it and came down with my other, severing its clawed hand from its leg. The beast howled in pain and fury.

"Heal that!" I challenged it.

The second beast was but a bound or two away from me, enraged that I had hurt the other one. Knowing my luck, they were mated pairs. Alpha had a knack for mating pairs of beasts, so he could breed them easier than having to recreate the bloodlines. I glanced at a rope above my head and debated the jump. I clicked the swords off and jumped, grabbing hold of the end. I kicked my legs, swinging myself up on a boulder. I kicked off from the height of the boulder and came down on the back of the beast I had severed the foot off. Midair, I activated the sword and buried it to the hilt in the monstrosity. It gave an enraged howl of pain before it teetered over. I twisted the blade, severing its spinal cord before ripping the blade from its back. As it hit the ground, I plunged the sword through the thing's sternum straight through its heart.

Before I had time to even appreciate the kill, the other monstrous creature roared with a bellowing rage that filled the quiet arena and sprinted toward me. I ran at full speed toward the creature, and just as it was about to pounce on me, I slid underneath it, holding the sword up, and drove the sword deep into its body. I sliced it clean open from the heart down to its stomach. Its innards fell out on top of me, and I was covered in the blood of the fresh kill. The body collapsed, dead to the arena floor. I walked up to the now dead beast and thrusted my hand into its chest cavity. I pulled its heart from the carcass and held it up to the crowd.

"Is that all you got?" I yelled, tossing the heart into the crowd.

Alpha smiled as the screech filled the arena. I turned to the source of the sound and watched as an enormous bird walked in from another of the open gates. Its beak was filled with razor sharp teeth like that of pterodactyls. It towered even taller than the werewolf mutts I had killed. It let out another deafening screech and spread its wings, flapping hard. The gusts of wind nearly toppled me over as it took to the sky. It had the wings of an angel, the body of a dragon, the face of a bird, and instead of just two sets of talons, it had four massive, clawed paws. Is that a… no. It can't be?

It was a mutated form of a gryphon. And, it had a great advantage right now. It was airborne. I sheathed my sword and pulled my bow from my shoulder. I clicked a button, and it spread into a large missile-shooting weapon as opposed to the puny bow it had appeared to be. I loaded one of the arrows and clicked a button on the side of it. It transformed into a huge spear. I drew the string of the bow back and let the arrow fly. It missed the bird mutt by inches. I drew another and another, shooting them as fast as I could. The bird taunted me in the air. It was planning the moment to strike, to swoop down and grab me up with its claws and rip me to shreds. The moment it thought I didn't have any more arrows, it would make its move.

No sooner had I thought the words than the bird swooped down to scoop up its prey. I rolled out of the way at the last minute and instantly readied the bow, releasing the spear into the back of the bird. It screeched in pain as it tore through the bone of its wing. It landed with a thud and turned to face me with a deafening sound that made me nearly grab my ears to drown out the debilitating noise. It ran for me, its tail growing longer and swiping my feet out from under me. It was on top of me, and I used my bow as a shield. It opened its mouth to take a bite, and I shoved the bow in. As it tried to shake the bow loose from its beak, I grabbed one of my swords and clicked it into action. With one sweep, as it brought its head down trying to drive its beak into my exposed torso, I sliced its head clean off. I quickly rolled out of the way as its body crashed onto the arena floor, spraying me with even more blood.

I stood from the ground and looked around the crowd as they sat silently. I picked the head of the beast up and thrusted it into the air. They erupted in cheers of my success. I tossed the head to the side and walked toward the center of the floor.

"Is that all?" I taunted. "I can do this for days!!!"

Alpha, looking none too pleased, just tapped his fingers together as a gong sounded. That was something new. What did the gong mean? Was it over? The ground shook as if an earthquake was splitting the arena in half. No, it wasn't over. It was the sound of hundreds of feet pounding on the arena floor, rushing to the center where I stood. They erupted from the gates all around me. All the creatures I had seen in the nightmare were now careening toward me in the middle of the stadium. Had I fallen unconscious at some point? Am I asleep? I blinked my eyes just to make sure this wasn't a dream. My eyes caught it just then. Within the piles of creatures spilling out, it was the beast that had angel wings and the distorted face with eyes that shone as bright as the sun. It moved in a clunky manner, almost as if it were an iron giant. I backed slowly away as the masses filled every gate except the one I had come through. My back touched the metal gate as they descended in on me. Snarling, drooling, growling, snapping mouths with teeth that dripped acid. Some had wings and were flying while others shot fire from their mouths. I tossed my sword to the ground to admit defeat. Alpha had won. I raised my arms as the crowd went nuts in terrified banter. I was giving up.

I felt the gate behind me shift, and just as the creatures were about to pounce, I was yanked through the gate with it thudding back shut.

"Now, did you really think we were going to let you die in there?" Incaendiel asked.

He dragged me away from the gate and out of the arena entrance, winding through the tunnels.

"But, how?" I began stammering.

"Less talking and more running!" he shouted.

He pulled me along the dark corridors as the sounds of the hungry creatures echoed through the hall.

"We have about three minutes before that gate is lifted and those things come after us," he said as he jerked me from hall to hall.

"How are you free?" I asked.

"Asmodeus is an old friend of mine. He has been filling me in on you for a few weeks. He told me about this, about what Alpha was going to do and how you refused to leave without setting me free," he replied. "Kid, what part of no one cares about themselves as much as they care about you three do you just not get?"

He pulled me down long corridors that I didn't recognize. Were we in a part that I had never been before?

"Where are you taking me?" I asked.

"To freedom," he answered.

He ran at full speed and busted through the wall ahead of him. As the dust settled, I looked around. It was the meadow just outside of my cell. Incaendiel stood blazing in the sun with his wings spread as wide as they could stretch. He looked like what a god should have looked like in that moment.

"Alpha is going to be hot on your trail," Incaendiel stated as he handed me a bag full of weapons. "You need to lead him on a wild goose hunt before you meet up with Xavier and Luxina. He's going to be sending everything he has your way, including those things he made to tear you apart. You have to be fast and remain strong."

"Aren't you coming with me?" I asked.

He shook his head. "I have someone else myself to save before I leave here," he replied.

Sophie.

"Yes, Sophie," he replied as if reading my mind. "Now, go! That's an order! I can take care of myself. There's an uprising. Alpha will have to flee. The Forsaken weren't too happy when they found out about this plan of his with you. You have friends in low places, kid."

"Make sure Asmodeus stays safe," I asked.

"You have my word," he replied. "Now, go!"

I didn't think twice about it. I was gone.

CHAPTER 7

I HAD NO TIME to cloak and run. If I needed to escape quickly and gain ground against the monsters, I had to fly. It began to rain as I took off from the ground, watching Incaendiel disappear back into the fortress we were held prisoner in together. I soared through the sky faster than a bolt of lightning striking, gaining momentum with each flap of my angelic wings. However, no matter how fast I flew, those things Alpha created were equally fast. I heard the screeches from behind me as a fleet of flying mutations pushed as hard as they could to catch up with me. With what bit of strength I had, I summoned the cooling ice from within me, and the rain that pelted down turned into shards of ice that could rip your flesh clean off your bones.

I heard the howls of pain as the ice bit into the

skin of the fleet following close behind me. I looked back to see each ice shard buried into the creatures, and they dropped one by one from the sky. Pleased with myself, I returned my attention to what was in front of me. Advancing toward me were more of the giant birds that I had fought in the arena. Their beaks bared their teeth as they screeched and howled with those same ear-splitting sounds that nearly caused me to falter from the sky. I didn't have time to grab any weapons from the bag that was draped over my shoulder. I held out my hand and shot ice spears from my palm. I couldn't even aim. I just pointed and blasted ice at them. They dipped and dodged from the onslaught of ice that I sent their way, still making their way headstrong toward me.

I didn't even think about my next action. I began to spin and twirl my body as I flew closer and closer to them. A whirlwind tunnel formed beneath my feet, and I stopped midair, continuing my spinning until the whirlwind grew into a twister. I held my hands out and blasted the sides of the funnel with ice as it picked up debris from the ground below. Ice weapons formed in the funnel, and the centrifuge suction of the winds pulled the birds into their impending demise. I stopped spinning and pushed the whirlwinds with my ice powers straight into their path. I could hear their screeches as the wind caught them and tore them to shreds with the sheets of icy winds.

Still, behind me, more creatures appeared, almost as if materializing from thin air. I used my palms and shot icy blockades that engulfed each of them one by one, and they dropped from the skies as frozen ice chunks. I continued to fly and shoot the ice as missiles at each of the targets that closed in on me. I was soon flying solo in the air once more and continued my ice storm for clear and safe passage through the skies.

A static filled the air as I forged my way through the falling crystals, immune to their blades of wrath. Even as the wind tore past me and the precipitation shot out at damaging speeds, silence fell all around me.

"Damian..." a voice whispered in the wind. *"Damian!"*

My eyes quickly surveyed my surroundings to see where the voice was coming from. It was a haunting, hollow voice.

"Damian!!" it bellowed. The sound echoed throughout the sky as I pushed forward harder and faster.

"Damian... you can run, but you can't hide from me..." the voice taunted me as I raced to find safety. Thunder rumbled, and lightning crackled all around me in the dark skies.

"I will always find you, Damian. There is nowhere you can go. Nowhere you can hide. No one that can keep

me from getting to you. And when I get to you, you're going to wish you had never been brought into this universe." The voice was smug, no doubt Alpha in one of his disillusioned states. "Just when you think you are free of me, I will be there to take your life myself. When you think you have won, I will be right there to show you your failures. You're mine, Damian. And if I can't have you at my side, then no one shall have you!"

A bolt of lightning careened through the air and struck me as I tried to dodge it. I was free-falling through the sky, half-conscious from the blast. One of my wings was torn and would no doubt need a long time of healing. I flexed with all my might but could not catch myself from somersaulting to the ground. My body went around and around as I grew closer and closer to the ground below. Tree tops came into view, and I hoped with everything in me that I could latch onto a branch before I thudded to my demise.

Almost as if by answer, as I came crashing through the trees, their limbs reached out, embracing me, grabbing me, and helping me slow down. I landed in a mound of moss with a softened thud. I lay there staring up into the canopy of trees, breathing deeply and rapidly as I tried to calm myself down from the adrenaline rush that had seized my body during the fall. All the trees erected back to the straightened trunks they had been before I descended. I sat up and checked the damage on my wing from the lightning. It was bleeding and burned badly, but I wouldn't lose it. I opened the weapon's bag to see if Incaendiel had stuffed any bandages in there for just in case purposes.

"I can fix that right up for you," a melodic voice rang out.

I looked around the trees to see where the voice had come from. My eyes rested on the last person I thought I would see anytime soon.

"Aren't you a little ways out of your kingdom?" I asked, standing to my feet.

Queen Mab moved from her shadowy spot in between the trees out to where I could see her better.

"I heard through the grapevine a certain Shining One needed my assistance. However, by the looks of things, I believe you have everything covered on your own," she replied with a sweet smile.

She looked different than the last time I had seen her. She looked my age as opposed to the middle-aged woman's body she had used when Alpha and I took court with her. She always had the most remarkable and astonishing features, no matter the body she assumed.

"So, the butterfly carried my message to you," I said, walking closer to her. "It's about several months too late."

"I'm afraid it wasn't safe for me to come directly

to Alpha's keep and take you away. But as I can see, someone did, in fact, help free you. Incaendiel, I presume?" she asked.

"Yeah, he was one of the last people I thought would help me bust out of there. I was sure he hated me for what I did under Alpha's control," I replied.

"Walk with me, love," she cooed, extending her arm out for me to loop mine through. "You have lots to learn about your friends."

I hesitated and looked around the field I had landed in. It was either go with her and have a little bit of protection from Alpha or wait here and see what other things he sent after me. I looped my arm through hers, and she walked me through the woods. Everything transformed before my eyes, and soon, we were surrounded by trees that had beautiful blooms falling from the branches. This must be the passageway to her court.

"Incaendiel is an old soul that my gods helped create," she murmured, passing by all her plants. They all reached out to touch her as she moved past them. She petted them as we walked. "Therein, you are much like me, as he is. You were born of the same universal power except far more superior."

"How are we more superior? What makes us so special?" I asked.

"You know how there are tons of angels that

Alpha and Omega created?" she asked, turning us to walk through a field of nightshade. The field peeled back as we walked through and closed behind us with each step we took. "Well, I am like that. We are the angels of our gods. The three of you were made with the power of the universe, not the power the gods possess. That is why starfire burns through your veins."

"I don't have fire in my veins, though. I have ice instead," I replied.

"Yes, because you are unique. I'm sure you have already stumbled across the prophecy in your studies," she presumed. "There must be a balance of power. You are the perfect complement of power to Luxina's fire."

"Then why wasn't I born as her twin flame? Xavier is her counterpart, not me," I replied.

"Who says you aren't her twin flame? They don't have to be born at the same time, you know?" she mused. "And you also know what must happen in the end. You know Luxina and you must absorb him with your powers. When you absorb him, you will each share a part of another with each other. She will have a touch of ice to her fire, and you will have a touch of fire to your ice," she explained.

I watched as her castle materialized down the path from us. Guards stood around the gates, armed to the teeth. Were they expecting a battle?

"That will never happen. It can't happen. I won't

do it," I replied. "In the end, we will all survive."

"If you do not do it, then the nightmare that riddles your dream will become the future. In order to save the universe, there must be sacrifice."

"Why can't I be the sacrifice?" I asked heatedly. "Why him?"

"You already know the answer as you have read it, and I have explained it. Xavier wasn't supposed to have been birthed. When Sophie and Incaendiel separated after raising the heavenly portal, the power of their creation was split in two as well. It was just supposed to be Luxina. Xavier was an accident. A fluke in the grand design. Finding the Garden of Eden wasn't the plan Omega had devised. That was just part of the game she played with Alpha. The real goal was to have Incaendiel and Sophie raise the heavenly portal. Only those two could have accomplished it, for they are gods greater than her and Alpha. She had to test their power. It was a rather cruel joke she played as well, making Incaendiel believe his darkness would kill Sophie if she stayed behind. But she couldn't keep them together. They were far too powerful together to control than they were apart. The whole sex part for to raise the Garden, well she wanted them to create Luxina. She is not as innocent as many believed her to be."

She walked us into her castle and led me to her

throne room.

"That last part doesn't surprise me," I replied. "We are all just pawns in their game."

"You are wise beyond your years, young Damian," she crooned as she sat down on her throne.

"So, what now? Do I stay here?" I asked.

"You may stay the night to recoup and mend your wing, but I am afraid the courts cannot protect you from Alpha," she replied gravely. "However, there is another option, but it is rather perilous."

"I'm running from danger. It makes sense to head straight into it as well," I chided.

"The Otherworld is a vast place outside of space and time. It has realms of its own buried within the magic that keeps it from collapsing in on itself. Alpha may be able to travel into the Otherworld; however, he cannot travel everywhere. Not even we Seelies travel into the realm of Shadows and Nightmares. It is nothing but darkness, and its name holds truth. It is where nightmares thrive. The ones that leach into your mind late at night are those that try to escape from the depths from which they were cast. There is no goodness that exists there. Unimaginable creatures creep and crawl much like those that Alpha has created with mutations."

"Is there any type of magical aid that can help me once I cross over into this place?" I asked.

"There are very, very few things, but I can

arrange for those that may aid you to be delivered for your journey. I will also include instructions on how to use them as well."

"Thank you for your kindness," I replied. "It is much needed and much appreciated."

Queen Mab motioned for one of her guards and whispered into his ear. He left the room and returned with another Seelie.

"This is Nautila. She will lead you to your quarters for the night. Rest well, Damian, for the future does not bring sleep for you," Queen Mab instructed with a dismissing hand.

Nautila curtsied before me, led me out of the throne room, and through the grand hall.

"Are you hungry?" Nautila asked.

I knew better than to eat faery food. They could trap you here with a single bite or drink of food.

"No, thank you," I replied.

She smiled as if she knew what I was thinking. "Queen Mab does not wish to keep you here as a slave. You have much to do to save not only your universe but our realm as well. Please, have something to eat."

She motioned me to a bountiful table of fruits, cheeses, and loaves of bread. There were chalices full of all kinds of meads, milks, and waters.

"Can you tell me what is ok for me to eat?" I asked nervously. "I know even though you can eat the food, it doesn't mean certain things will not harm me."

She nodded and gathered some food on a plate for me. She placed some bread and cheese on the plate, skipping the fruit. She grabbed me a chalice of water and led me off from the room. The castle buzzed with fey both sleeping and awake. Some danced merrily as music was played, while others sat in groups listening to sonnets being recited. It was amazing the candor they had, knowing they may be wiped from existence.

Nautila wound up a stairway and banked to the left down a long corridor. She pushed a door open on her right and led me into a quaint room. She sat the plate of food and chalice down on the table at the door. I looked for a lamp but then realized there wasn't any type of artificial lighting here. She smiled, guessing I was looking for lighting. She walked over to a makeshift lamp and opened a door in it. She gently blew inside of it, and dozens of fireflies lit up inside it. She closed the door, and the light grew brighter.

"Thank you for your hospitality," I said graciously with a bow.

"Is there anything else you may need?" she asked, leaning her shoulder seductively against the door frame. "Lonely?"

I eyed her as she stood before me at the door. She was petite and wearing a dress made from moss and flowers. Every inch of her clothing clung to just the right parts of her body, adding a mystifying allure to her. How do I respectfully decline this?

"I am fine. Again, I thank you for everything," I replied with a smile.

She curtsied and left the room, closing the door behind her. I expected to hear a lock come down in place, as I had always heard in the dungeon. I didn't hear a click. I walked to the door and tried the knob, and it opened freely. I reclosed the door and slumped down in the chair at the table. I eyed the food, both hungry and nauseated. I picked up a bit of cheese and some bread and nibbled at them. I drank from the chalice of water until it was empty. I hadn't realized how thirsty I was. I tried to think of the last time I had eaten and drunk something, but my mind was so jumbled with the events of the day that it was a futile effort. As I set the chalice back down on the table, it magically filled with more water just as cool as the water I had drank. They thought of everything here. Never-ending food, never-ending water; it was a neverland of wants and needs.

A wave of exhaustion overtook me, and I threw myself on the bed near the open window. It was soft with moss and ivy for a blanket. I lay on top of the moss and stared out of the window. The sky dazzled with its own little solar system of stars and planets. Unlike on Earth, where you can't see the planets, just bright dots in the sky, the planets were up close here and marvelously breathtaking. It felt as if I was back at the Summit all over again.

I remembered how the galaxy sparkled and lit up everywhere with stars and dust particle clouds hued in blues, pinks, and purples. The sky here was not dark but a dark shade of pink and purple. A moon rose gallantly through the sky, a light bluish glow illuminating it. It was peaceful, serene. I sat waiting for the door to bust open and guards to rush forward to bring me to some torture chamber as I had been accustomed to it for so long. However, no one came, and I was able to lie in bed in a somber state.

My mind wandered, and I found myself thinking about the prophecy, about what the Dark Queen had told me. There was no doubt that Lilith was as sly as Alpha and equally manipulative. She was his other half after all. But, to subject Incaendiel and Sophie to the lies she had was unforgivable. Even as much as she helped, she couldn't be trusted in the slightest. Did she know about the prophecy and what the birth of Luxina and Xavier meant? If she had just let Incaendiel be with Sophie, would there be this issue at hand right now? I felt like I was grappling with my own fate when, in fact, I was grappling with the idea of life without Xavier. I thought back to Queen Mab's words, and they made complete sense. Xavier is the dark half of Luxina's soul, an extension of

113

everything she felt, thought, and existed to be. Did he know it? Had he figured out that he wasn't supposed to exist in this life?

I remembered watching them in that field in our dreams. The first time they ever met, when they touched, it leveled the field with power. Luxina's power was trying to reattach, but the momentum of the touch instead made the power reflect itself back. I sighed heavily. I didn't like this prophecy, and if we didn't do as it dictated, then the apocalyptic vision I had would manifest in the end. In that vision, we all three stood before Alpha but were powerless against him. Would we three be selfish enough to end everything, let the universe crumble in on itself just to exist as we were born? It was unfair to ask us to do such things. It was even more unfair to lay all this on Xavier's shoulders. I couldn't blame him one bit if he chose to let the universe end. Luxina and I wouldn't even flinch at that decision and would try everything we could to reverse the possible outcome of the end times. But if he chose to do it… If he chose to sacrifice himself for the good of the universe, he would need to be immortalized in some shape or form. He wouldn't even be given a grave at Potter's Field because his soul would just be absorbed.

I have become so tired of the power trip of the gods and the mess they have created with everyone involved. People I love dearly are having to make life and death decisions like kings and queens. We were kids, and we're faced with things that shouldn't even be thought about. Our creators were supposed to be gods, and they acted as mortals would with greed, envy, and jealousy, almost as if they were the epitome of the seven deadly sins themselves. Their selfishness was the downfall of this universe and the reason it was caving in on itself. Their selfishness was causing all of us grief and despair. We shouldn't have to turn on them to make things right. They should know how to do it themselves.

I closed my eyes, but not for long. My thoughts drifted off back to the arena, back to those creatures all swarming me. The iron giant angel that Alpha had created. Was that the diagram I had seen in his office? Were they able to syphon from my blood the magic to bring those things to life? There would be no stopping them if they were let loose. My eyes did not mistake the shimmering glow of metal. And if they were made of iron... I remembered Queen Mab telling Alpha that he was unable to harm her. Could those things destroy the Otherworld as well? Is that why they were so damning to us, to Luxina, Xavier, and me? Because we were a superior race to the fey but made by the same power, just an amplified amount, is that why those things could destroy us?

I thought back to the enhanced werewolf Alpha

115

had created and the dripping acid saliva. Maybe there was more to it than it being acid. Maybe... oh no! I bolted upright in my bed and clamored to get up. I opened the door of my room and ran down the long corridor. I wound down the stairs, bounded through the great hall, and entered the throne room where the Dark Queen rested.

"You're in danger, and you need to flee to safety. All you," I stammered.

Queen Mab smiled. "I have already sent all those in the Unseelie court to Titania and Oberon for safety."

"Why did you stay behind? You are in danger!" I yelled. "You need to go!"

"I promised you some things that you need prior to voyaging through the Nightmares and Shadows realm," she replied. A guard walked in carrying my bag. "Ah, right on time, Ceri. Thank you, join the others."

The guard nodded and disappeared down the hall.

"Here is your bag of weapons and also the weapons I promised you to help," she said, handing me the bag that Incaendiel had given me. "We modified the swords you had in there. They are now encased with iron and silver."

She stood from her throne and began to walk through the long hall. She turned around and

116

motioned for me. "Come along, Damian. I will show you where the entrance to the realm is, and then I will be on my way."

I followed her down the long hall where guards lined the walls. These guards looked different compared to the ones I had seen when we first arrived. They were dressed differently.

"These are my foot soldiers, my warriors," she replied. "They are specially trained in unique battle techniques."

I hope they are. If I was right about Alpha's creations...

The howl came with a deafening crack through the air of the castle.

"We must hurry," Queen Mab stressed, grabbing my arm and towing me faster through the castle.

We exited the keep with her little army of warriors on our heels. I could hear the pounding of the feet of the creatures Alpha had sent into this realm. He was starting a war that he intended no one to survive.

"There are vials of poisons in your bag, as well as silver flakes, and a special powder I blended from Forget-Me-Trees to make invisible creatures appear to you. They forget why they are invisible when it is used. There are several other things with the instructions, just as I promised."

We were running as fast as we could down the path.

"Take the next right, Damian. And may the universe keep you safe. This is as far as I can go. I must get to the safety of the Seelie court," Queen Mab said, pointing down a path up on my right. "Go, my boy!"

And with a shove of her hand, she sent me in the direction of the path to the Nightmares and Shadows realm of the Otherworld.

CHAPTER 8

I WAS LOST in total darkness, wandering a road that I had no clue where it ended. They didn't call this place the Nightmares and Shadows realm for no reason. It was exactly that. It was even harder keeping track of time in this place than it had been in the Otherworld. The darkness stretched on for miles with the crackle of lightning and the rumble of thunder here and there. With each step I took, the ground slightly glowed underneath my feet, almost as if the road itself was alive. That's exactly what I needed right now, to be swallowed by a living creature disguised like a sunfish. However, I pushed forward. Those things Alpha had created knew absolutely zero boundaries regarding their own mortality or lack thereof. They would follow me in here and wreak havoc upon me and anything else that was in their way.

Streaks of blue cut across the sky that I could only surmise were shooting stars in the desolate abyss that hung above me. Voices swirled around me, almost as if ghosts of the past tiptoed around down here. It almost looked as if memories in my head were playing on a screen as I walked through hazy forms of people. Every evil thing I had ever done played on repeat through the sky for me to watch. The length of Alpha's control over me haunted me as I was forced to remember everything I had done to Luxina and Xavier. I saw my face with my eyes blacked over as I whisked Luxina away from Incaendiel. My face as I fought with Xavier after Lucifer brought him to me. I tried so hard to be nice and loving, but Alpha and those injections turned me into a monster.

That's what I was and most likely still am, Alpha's little monster. I don't want to be. I want to be good. I want to be pure like Luxina is. The deeper I walked, the more scenes unfolded before me of every single little thing that had happened to me. Was there ever a time that I had more than just an inky black depth to my soul? Did I ever have a technicolor to me that separated me from the weapon Alpha had been molding into me? I had learned my lesson, whether at fault or not, for the assailing attacks I had inflicted upon masses in the name of Alpha. But were those bridges burned long turned to dust and able to rebuild back? Or are they still burning in anger and hatred toward me?

It felt as if no one would ever know me for who I truly was and not the puppet Alpha had made me into. Even Incaendiel had his doubts about me. He would continue to have those doubts, too, until I could prove myself to him that I was worthy of the light and not the suffocating shadows that grappled with me internally. No amount of hiding would ever erase the damage I had caused throughout the universe. There were so many silent sorrows lost in the yesterdays of my existence that I didn't even know what tomorrow promised me. There wasn't a promise of forgiveness, a promise of love, or promises of wholeness.

If there were any moments that could have meant something, they were now gone. Pieces of chaos were all that was left, blowing on the wind from the aftermath of my storm. Could I ever prove myself to Luxina that I was more than this creature I had become? Would she ever love me for me? See my true inner light? Could she see the colors that existed within me that I could not even see?

Damian, the voice whispered. I looked around to see if anyone was following me. It was nothing but darkness as far as my eyes could see.

Damian, come for me, it whispered again. I began to panic just a bit. The voice sounded like Luxina's voice, but I couldn't be sure. Was she down here? Was she hurt?

"Luxina!" I called out. "Luxina, where are you?"

Daaaamiannnn, the voice sang. *Come for me, Damian. I need you.*

"Where are you?" I implored, a sickly anxiety building deep in my stomach. "Why are you here? Tell me where you are, and I will find you."

And then, I saw her. She was about fifty yards out, standing in the middle of the path I was walking. I began to run to her, but the more I ran, the further away she seemed to be.

"Luxina, run to me," I urged out. "It's not safe here."

No, it isn't, she whimpered, her voice caught up in the violent winds that began to tear at the foundation of the road. *Save me, Damian.*

"I'm trying," I sputtered, breathless and desperate.

Save me before it's too late. Save me before I turn into stardust floating through the universe, she wailed, her voice distant and distorted.

I ran hard and fast, inching closer and closer to her outstretched hand. A sword sliced through the middle of her chest, and blood spilled down the front of her torso.

"No!" I screamed, stumbling and hitting the ground.

She fell to her knees and dematerialized, bits of dust dispersing all around me.

Damian, another voice called out.

Panic now riddled every breath I tried to suck in as my heartbeat quickened with every gasp. My chest tightened in fear as I looked for the owner of the voice because I knew it too. My eyes scanned around the darkness, looking for Xavier.

Damian, why do you hate me? he warbled. *Why do you want me to die?*

"I don't want you to die," I cried, pounding the ground before me.

You are the reason Alpha wants me. You are the reason Alpha has me, he argued.

"No," I whispered. "It's not real."

Save me, Damian. Save me before Alpha kills me. Save your brother from eternal damnation, he crowed.

I glanced up to see Xavier standing ten feet from me. His hand reached for mine, and I lifted mine from the ground, stretching for his hand. He was dragged backward by an invisible force. He clawed and clamored, trying to break himself free.

Damian! You must save me! he hollered. *You must save Luxina!*

He was pinned to the ground. I scrambled to try and reach him, but the distance between us grew in leaps and bounds the harder I tried to reach him.

"I'm trying!" I screamed, my voice cracking from the pressure of the words exerted on my vocal cords. "I am trying so hard to keep you safe. I am trying so hard to save you both."

Damian, help us! he screamed.

I looked up just in time to see his head lopped from his body and roll across the grass, stopping inches in front of me. Blood sprayed me as my hands shook with fury and pain. I tried to wipe the blood from my hands and face, but the more I wiped, the more it seemed to spread and stick. I frantically smeared them across my clothes, and it seemed that nothing I did was helping. I put my fists against my ears, squeezed my eyes tightly shut, and let out a guttural scream as I rocked back and forth. When I had no breath left to continue, I opened my eyes. Xavier had dematerialized. I looked at my hands and clothes, inspecting them for blood, but not a drop was on them.

I felt like I was suffocating.

What are you doing, boy!

"It's not real," I mumbled, crying into my fists.

Did you think you could hide from me? I always know where you are. You can never hide from me! the voice yelled, the voice of Alpha.

"This isn't real," I repeated. "This isn't real. This isn't real."

You are nothing more than what I have made you to

be. You will always have evil in you, no matter how hard you fight it. You will always be a creature. You will always be my monster.

"No!" I shouted. "No, I will not! I am not a monster!"

You think you are so smart. You think you are stronger than me, but you are nothing but a weak, little boy that will always search for people to love him. Not a single person will ever care for you. You are unlovable. I made sure of it. I have left you riddled in scars that leave you hideous to look at. I have turned your heart black and cold to anyone that dared to save you from me. I made sure that you couldn't slip through my fingers. I made sure love could never save you.

"No!"

Love is weak. Love isn't real. It's an illusion that pulls you into an imaginary land of wonder. It will begin to fade until it completely disappears, leaving you in writhing agony, leaving you in a pit of anguish that you can't breathe in. Do you think she will stay once she sees you for who you really are? She will go away. She won't want you when she sees the monster deep within.

"No, you're wrong. Love is patient and kind and everything that she is," I barked back.

Do not quote my scripture at me, boy! There is nothing but a cold, empty decay in you. And you will only ever feel it as it eats away at you, as it eats away at everything you love until there is nothing left but darkness and ruin. You are nothing but a monster, a soldier in a war that ends in death for those you hold

125

tightly to. You are MY monster, and you will obey your Master!

"I won't let you win," I refuted. "I will always fight against you. You will never own me. You never did!" I shouted.

Laughter filled the air. Thousands of creatures swarmed me as I pulled my sword to fight them off. I didn't even look as I slashed and hacked through the barrage of monsters that came at my left, right, front, and back. A mountain of bodies formed around me as they increased in numbers. When I began to pay attention to what I was fighting in the darkness, I dropped my sword and pushed my way through the bleeding bodies. They weren't the creatures I thought. Angels lay in heaps around me. My face reflected in their armor, and I could see the black eyes of death staring back at me. I howled in rage. No matter where I ran, Alpha would be there. I was a monster trained to kill. Even the monsters in my head were real and heavily trained to kill me. There was no escape. There was no respite.

I heaved and heaved all the contents of my stomach to the ground, then dropped my sword with a clatter, falling to my knees. I bent over, placing my head to the ground, wallowing and crying in defeat. A tug came at my arm.

"Mister?" a little voice asked.

"Something else that isn't real," I asserted to myself.

I looked down to see an exceedingly small child-like being standing beside me. She was dressed like one of the fey, but her skin color was a dark shade of blue.

"Oh, I am real alright," the itty-bitty thing replied. "Why are you here? This place isn't for you."

"I have to be here," I explained.

"But you walked into the Bog of Damnation," she replied. "If you stay here, you will surely die. It turns every one of your nightmares, grievances, and fears to life until you can't handle it anymore."

"What?" I asked.

I looked around as my eyes came into focus. The darkness that had encased me began to slowly fade into some form of watery grave.

"Come with me," she smiled. "I can show you safer places to travel while here in the shadows."

She offered me her hand, and I stood as she led me away from the decaying cypress trees and mosh pits.

"My name is Nillona," she stated. "And you are?"

"Damian," I replied.

"It is nice to make your acquaintance, Damian," she responded cheerfully. "You must be the one everyone has been talking about," she declared as we walked through a small forest.

"What do they say?" I asked.

"That you're going to save the universe," she replied. "That you are important, and everyone should make sure you make safe passage through here on your journey."

"Is that so?" I asked.

"Mhmm," she squeaked.

"What makes them think I am anything more than a monster?" I asked.

"Because Queen Mab helped you escape into the realm," she replied. "Although we live in an untethered part of the kingdom, a lot of us do respect Queen Mab's decisions in her rule."

"Why do you live here and not in Unseelie court?" I asked as she led me in what seemed like circles through the woods.

"Those who live here do not wish to be forced into a governing rule. We aren't all pure evil. There are some creatures here that are the essence of evil, but the others just want to exist without being told what we can and cannot do. We were all once loyal followers to Mab until she started her own personal war with the Seelie court. Bickering is not becoming of fey," she replied quietly. "So many of us retired to the shadows. Shadows aren't always bad. They are just a subtle reminder that light now exists."

"You are a very wise little girl," I mused.

"Well, I may be small, but I am not a girl," she rebutted. "I am 362 years old. I have seen and heard things as well as taught things."

She gave a soft giggle as my face flushed.

"My apologies, little lady," I digressed.

"No need for apologies, lad," she insisted. "No use in fretting over little things."

She led me to a tiny, quaint village tucked away safely inside the forest. Cottages with smoke billowing from chimneys sat spaced apart with gardens in between each. Many of the villagers sat gathered around a fire, singing and dancing, when we came walking up. A few of them had instruments that they gayly played. Silence filled the air as they paused the merriment and stared at me while I equally stared back.

"He is not to be harmed," Nillona instructed those sitting within hearing distance. "Make sure everyone knows, or there will be consequences."

They all nodded their acknowledgement of the declared immunity of my head on a platter.

"Not to be harmed? Would they harm me if not for your protection order?" I asked.

"Oh, yes. We are Gwyllion. We are normally tricksters, but tonight, we shall be hospitable," she replied smiling. "Please, sit and eat with us. I promise you. We will not poison you."

I nodded my thanks and squatted beside the fire, warming my hands up by the crackling embers. I couldn't help but feel a nagging sensation tug at the back of my brain. Could I really trust them? They were pretty upfront about what kind of fey they were but ensured that they meant no harm. However, I couldn't help but think that I would wake in the morning being handed over to Alpha.

"You're nothing but skin and bones," Nillona said. "Here, eat up and get some fat back on you."

Correction, I could wake up being eaten. She handed me some sort of dish that I could only guess had meat on it. My stomach turned just looking at the food. I looked over at the other Gwyllions as they used their bare hands to pick the food up and tear into it. Juices dripped from the mouths that they chomped loudly from. I swallowed the nausea building and set the plate down.

"I can't eat, but thank you," I replied.

"Mind if I have it?" a chubby Gwyllion asked.

"Knock yourself out," I replied, pushing the plate to him. Nillona eyed me. "I haven't eaten much in so long that the smell of food makes me sick to my stomach."

Her eyes softened. "So, the rumors of your torture are true as well?" she asked.

I nodded. "Alpha used me to do his dirty work, and whether I was to succeed or fail, I was punished to the full extent."

"That explains all the hideous scars," she said, pointing to my face. "A face only a mother would love," she chided.

I didn't expect her words to bite, but they did. I had never been self-conscious before, but knowing that I was now littered with scars made me feel tiny.

"I didn't mean no harm," she cooed. "It was a terrible thing to say, and I apologize."

"It's ok," I replied. "I am just starting to come to terms with how awful I must look."

"Whoever chooses to love you will love you for more than what you look like on the outside. My understanding is that you have a heart of gold. That will be the breadwinner with any decent woman," she gushed, nodding in agreement with herself. "Anyone special in your life? A girl waiting for you?"

"Maybe, maybe not," I replied.

"Well, which is it. Out with it," she prodded.

"At this moment, I don't know. She doesn't know a lot of things and probably just sees me as the monster I was made to be," I replied.

"If she thinks of you as a monster, then she is a monster herself," Nillona stated. "It is mighty fine what you are doing for the creatures of the universe that have neither helped you nor defended you in the years past. We all owe you a debt for what you are doing."

"What exactly am I doing?" I asked, still not knowing what the rumors were swirling around. "What have you heard through the grapevine, so to speak?"

"Why, bringing down Alpha, of course," she replied. "It has been many a year that he has stolen fey from the Otherworld and used the blood from their corpses to run experiments on humans."

"On humans?" I asked, sitting forward. "That I did not know."

"Aye," she replied. "He has been turning humans into creatures of darkness, his Children of the Night."

"What kind of creatures has he made?" I asked.

"Vampires, for starters," she began.

"Everyone knows about the vampires," I replied, shaking my head.

"No, young one. You know about the vampires he made trying to make humans. You don't know of the vampires he has made using humans. It isn't right, I tell ya. Poor souls. Trapped in darkness they are. The sunlight burns their skin to a crisp if exposed. If they stand in it too long, they burst into flames," she said. "Plus, the only thing they can eat is blood."

"What else has there been?" I asked.

"The easier question is what has there not been," she replied grimly. "He took the werewolves and changed humans into those as well. Unlike the full moon shifters, these ones shift into wolves whenever they want to or whenever they can't control themselves. Sometimes their anger makes them shift against their will."

"So, he just kidnaps mortals and subjects them to his tests?" I asked. "How could I not know this?"

"He has been doing it for centuries, love," she replied. "Long before you were ever born."

A few of the Gwyllion were whispering amongst themselves motioning to me, which undoubtedly made me uneasy.

"They want to know if you will demonstrate your power for them," Nillona disclaimed. "We heard tell that you have special powers no other angel has."

I picked up a cup in front of me that had water in it and dipped my finger in it. The water began to turn to ice instantly. The Gwyllions murmured and chattered quietly amongst themselves. I removed my finger from the cup and dumped the lump of ice onto the ground.

"So, the legends are true?" Nillona asked. "You really are one of the Shining Ones."

I nodded my head in affirmation.

"And the young woman you were speaking of, she is the one from the prophecy too, right?" she asked.

"Yes," I replied. "But I have been mirrored as a monster to her by Alpha, so she probably hates me."

"Word has it that she was adamant about saving you from Alpha and even asked Queen Mab to help as well," Nillona mused.

"Really?" I asked, a bit baffled.

"Aye, especially after Queen Mab said you would need to be killed if Alpha's injections were successful on you," Nillona responded.

"The only thing she told Alpha was if he was successful that I belonged to her," I replied.

"That was so Alpha wouldn't have you as a weapon. However, she knew Alpha had no intention of turning you over to her. That is why she executed a kill order in case your injections did turn you into a beast," she hissed.

"Well, I guess it's a good thing I escaped him then, huh?" I asked.

"That's enough chit-chat for one night," Nillona said, abruptly standing to her feet. "Let me show you where you can rest your head for the night."

I stood from the ground and followed her to one of the tiny cottages at the end of the row of houses.

"This one is empty. You can stay as long as you would like," she said with a nod to her head.

"Thank you, it is much appreciated. I can't stay too long, though. I don't want to put you all in any danger," I replied graciously.

"We can handle our own. You need not worry about that," she said with a sharp nod of her head and turned on her heel, walking away.

I ducked into the cottage that was about a foot

too short for me to stand straight up in. There wasn't much to the place. It had a bed, and that was pretty much it. I took my weapons bag off my shoulder and tossed it on the bed, and my body followed. I had no clue how long I had been walking in this place before she came along, but I knew I was tired. I feared sleep more than I feared dying here. There was no telling what kind of dreams I would have after experiencing what I did in the Bog of Damnation. Everything had felt and looked so real... just like the apocalyptic dreams I had.

My skin crawled just thinking about those visions of how the end played out. I rubbed my hands up and down my arms, feeling each and every bump, scar, and scab from what Alpha had put me through. My thoughts roamed to my conversation with Nillona regarding how I looked now with the scars riddling every inch of my skin. They would never go anywhere and always would be visible to everyone. *A face only a mother could love...* she was right. The few times I had caught sight of myself in a reflection, I looked absolutely hideous. My once smooth, creamy skin was now littered with pink whip marks from my abuse at Alpha's hands. Sometimes, the whip would peel my skin back, so there were large lumps of flesh that had to heal that way, leaving jagged edges on some of the scars. Whether it was real in the bog or not, the things he had said to me were true. He had made me unlovable by making me unbeautiful. Luxina would never look at me as she does Xavier. I am not beautiful in the least now. I am an eyesore to gaze at.

A girl waiting for you? I never even considered if Luxina had any type of feelings toward me at all. The few times we had any interaction, I was under the duress of Alpha. If I had shown her any type of compassion or empathy, or even if I had shown her that I was not evil, had she seen it? She must have. *She was adamant about saving you.* Why would she want so desperately to save me? The only thing I could surmise is to protect the universe. Could it be more than that, though? Could she have suppressed feelings for me? Feelings she didn't even acknowledge because she knew what happens when you abandon your twin flame?

Sophie did a number on all of us regarding the psychological destruction she caused by not staying true to Incaendiel. We all walked on eggshells, wondering if this was really the path that fate had spelled out for us when it came to whom we loved. In the end, Sophie chose Incaendiel as her one true love, and he made her go to protect her. Lilith's cruel punishment to keep their power apart had damaged this family in ways that it would be a miracle to mend the bonds. *Family…* Did I think of them all as my family? Could there be a time in the future when I can look to Sophie as my mother? My creator? I guess only time would tell at this point.

I sighed deeply while closing my eyes, trying to do anything but think of Luxina, but it was a failed attempt. There was no doubt that I had always loved Luxina, but it had always been a protective sort of love. I had never wanted to intercede between Xavier and her. However, I can't help but wonder if I had always had an interest in her. Alpha was pushing me to do to her what he had done to Sophie for all those years. Had he known this whole time about the prophecy? Had he done what he did with Sophie and Lucifer to bring about the prophecy? It was nauseating to think he would have done this all on purpose just to have us as a war machine for him. However, knowing the truth about Luxina and Xavier now, I can't help but to look deeper into how I feel about Luxina, developing Alpha's original plot without intending to do so.

I can't help but wonder if she will or does feel the tug at her heartstrings for me as well. Can she truly give up Xavier to be with me? Most likely not. Who would sacrifice love just to save me, to save the universe?

Could it be possible to be in love with two people at the same time and be able to choose one over the other? She was adamant about my safety... did she love me? If they were presented the prophecy, would they eagerly climb aboard? Would one fight it and the other accept it? Which one would fight it, and which one would accept it? So many questions swarmed through my mind. When Luxina is told about the prophecy, would she choose me out of obligation or because she really wanted me? That was the million-dollar question. I had no idea if she would ever love me in the capacity she had loved Xavier, even after finding out that Xavier was just the dark half of her soul made sentient. There's also the possibility she could resent me for having to give him up. There's also the possibility that she would choose not to choose me in the end.

How do you tell someone that the person they love is really their shadow self and it was a cruel joke of the universe for her to love him? Was it a joke, though? Incaendiel had grappled with his darkness for so many years, nearly succumbing to the darkness many times. Was she given a chance to love the dark half of herself, so she wouldn't be so easy to slip into the inky black depths of the abyss in her mind?

I tossed and turned, unable to fall asleep after plaguing myself with every question imaginable to think of to further my anxiety over the situation. I laid my head on the pillow, and my feet hung off the short bed. Feelings for Luxina were growing in me that were unstoppable at this point, and I didn't know how to slow them down. It wasn't hard to feel them once they began to blossom. Luxina was breathtaking. Her eyes could stare straight into your soul. I rolled to my side and began to drift off. Sleep was arriving, whether I wanted it, needed it, or wanted nothing to do with it.

Screams erupted from outside of the cottage that ripped me from my half-dozing thoughts and had me grabbing for my weapon bag, tossing it over my shoulder. I pulled a sword from within and walked to the door. No sooner had I reached the door handle, it popped open, and Nillona was standing there.

"The trackers have found you," she panted, alarmed. "You need to go!"

"I cannot leave you all unprotected," I protested, stepping through the door and outside. "They are here because of me. I will fight to protect those who showed me hospitality."

"It is a noble notion, young Damian, but it is you we must protect, even if we die trying," she refuted hastily. "Now, take this map." She handed me a folded-up piece of parchment paper. "Slip off behind the trees and keep running in a straight line. You will come across a riverbank. Follow the riverbank east. The map will show you everything you need to know to maneuver through the shadows and how to get to where you need to go. Use this to light your way as well," she said, slipping a rock into my hand.

"I can't thank you enough," I replied with a bow, slipping the paper and rock into my pants pocket.

"Go, Shining One. And when there are those that ask you how you were able to manage through the Nightmares and Shadows, you tell them. You tell them Nillona of the Gwyllions helped you. You honor my name," she spouted, pushing me off into the woods.

"You have my word," I replied in a shout as I took off into the woods.

I did what she said. I stayed in a straight line as I ran through the woods, branches whipping me in the face. Vines seemed to reach from places unknown to snag me and try to pull me down. I pushed through it all. I ran with every ounce of energy I had, escaping the screams and howls of pain coming from the village behind me. They were dying for me. They were dying to save the universe, and I had to make sure that people knew exactly who it was that helped me, just as Nillona asked. I wouldn't let anyone who helped me and perished die in vain. The universe would know each name and would worship them for eons to come.

The trees opened directly in front of a river just as she had said they would. I pulled the map from my pocket and folded it open. Not only had she provided me with a means of traveling through this hellish place, but she also gave me a tiny rock that glowed in the dark. I had wondered what the rock would do when she thrust it into my hands. I adjusted the weight of the weapons bag and held the light over the paper. She said to head east. I scoured the map and a tiny, red x appeared on the map with "you are here" written underneath it.

"Show me east," I stated.

Little red dots began to emerge on the map to the left of the x on the page. I turned in the direction the map led me, and as I walked, the x moved. The dots closest to the x would disappear and new ones would appear in the forefront. I looked closely at the name of the river listed on the map I was following. *River of Sorrows* was what it was called. *I wonder what that meant?* I know how the Bog of Damnation was dangerous. I wonder if this place was as dangerous. I glanced at the river, but it just looked like a normal river to me. I shrugged my shoulders and continued what I had been doing.

I scanned the map, looking for landmarks that were named that I would come across following this river. All along the river were strange names for specific spots. There was *The Hanging Tree, Dead Man's Leap,* and *Bleeding Hearts Forge.* It dawned on me what the river really implicated, and I came to a complete stop. It was a suicide river. I slowly turned my head to look closer at the running water and quickly snapped it back, squeezing my eyes shut. Bodies piled on one another all along the riverbank, the boulders in the river, and some floated freely along the river current. This was where the fey came to kill themselves. How could I not have seen the bodies the first time? Did you have to be aware of what the river was like in order to see them?

I breathed deeply, slowly letting the air out of my lungs and gently breathing back in. I tried to calm my nerves and made myself trudge forward, keeping my eyes on the path ahead of me. I had enough images of bloated, dead bodies to keep me awake for centuries now, added along with the creatures Alpha made and every single other thing that plagues my mind.

I stayed on the path that the map pointed out to me, walking closer to the first place on the map, which was called *The Hanging Tree*. Voices began to whisper in the wind, and for a moment, terror took hold of my stomach as it knotted, remembering how the Bog of Damnation had drawn me in. I glanced up from the map briefly to see translucent lines of fey heading in single file lines to the riverside. Up ahead was a tall, incredibly old tree. The base of the trunk was at least fifty feet wide, and its branches reached tall into the dark sky, almost as if touching the clouds from below. The whispers turned into an audible lull as they sang the saddest song I had ever heard as they marched forth to the tree.

THE TREE TWISTS high
The tree twists low
Follow me,
Follow me, oh
Down the forgotten path
Of nameless peace
To the hanging tree
Where a necklace
Of silvery fire
Hoists you up over
A deathly mire
No screams come out
As you descend
From the hanging tree

I WATCHED as they disappeared and reappeared hanging from the branches of the tree. Their bodies swung back and forth in the wind. I stood, horrified and yet mystified, at the grandeur of the entire scene. Their song called to me in a bittersweet memento of a certain promised death. Death... I wanted death. I craved death like a butterfly craved the sweet nectar produced within the buds of wildflowers growing in meadows. I craved it like a caged fox craves the sweet escape of captivity to run boundlessly free, jumping and twisting in the air, running after the butterfly. I had craved it for so long I could taste what it felt like. The sweet reprieve washing over my body as it slowly turned to stardust in the wind.

I don't know what it was that snapped me from the lull I had been placed in. It sounded like someone calling my name to get my attention. As I snapped back to lucidity, I stood upon a branch of the Hanging Tree with a noose wound tightly around my neck. The tree had called me to death, and I had blindly followed the path it had rolled out before me. I tore the noose from around my neck and jumped from the tree branch, thudding to my behind on the muddy riverbank. I scrambled back over to the path as fast as I could. I searched for the map, hoping I hadn't dropped it, and it floated away in the wind. I patted myself down and pulled the map out from my pocket. I didn't even remember putting it in there prior to climbing the tree.

I briskly walked from the tree and continued on down the road, putting distance between me and my near, ill-fated brush with death. I now understood why Queen Mab had declared this place dangerous. It wasn't so much as creatures as the actual realm trying in a whole to dispatch whoever didn't belong here. Nightmares and Shadows was a ravenous creature in itself. It was starved of fresh blood and was pushing as hard as it could to get me to take my own life here. Twice now, it had nearly succeeded. Had I not been pulled from the Bog of Damnation, I most surely would have taken my own life then as well.

More quiet voices floated to my ears as I saw the fey spirits pour from the woods, rushing as quickly as they could to the river and throwing themselves into the murky depths. I waited for each of them to surface, but none ever did. It explained the bodies upriver where the water was shallower than what it was here. Their song grew in volume as I struggled to ignore it.

WE'RE MARCHING on
Down to the river
We move as one
Down to the river
The noose hangs low
Down at the river
The water runs cold
Down at the river
Our souls shall roam
Down by the river

Forsaken ashore
Down by the river
Our bodies are drawn
Down through the river
Time won't move on
Down through the river
We're marching on
 Down to the river
We move as one
Down to the river...

THE SONG CONTINUED, and it soon became amplified by the growing voices of the dead. I quickened my pace so I wouldn't get lost in the soulful songs and follow them along into the cold waters of death they disappeared into. How long did this river go on for? Did it just end, or did it turn into a waterfall? The map gave no indication of how far or how long I was supposed to follow the river. I didn't even know where I was supposed to be going. She just told me to follow the river. Follow the river to where? No one told me where I was supposed to go while in this realm.

A peaceful serenity overcame me. I could hear sweet sounds floating in the air like the sound of rain in the mountains during a summer storm.

AAAAAAAAAHHHHHH, Aaaaaaaaaaaahhhh

I LOOKED for the source of the melodic notes and saw Luxina standing near the riverbank, swinging from a tree branch, feet kicking back and forth in the air.

"Luxina?" I called out.

She looked back at me and smiled, giggles erupting in the breeze. Her mouth opened, and the beautiful notes I had heard poured from her lips.

AAAAAAAAAHHHHHH, Aaaaaaaaaaaahhhh

I WALKED CLOSER TO HER, drawn in by everything. The sun beat down on her hair, and it looked like tendrils of fire whipping back and forth as her hair blew in the breeze. Her smile drew me in, and I felt compelled to watch her, leaning against the tree she swung back and forth from.

AAAAAAAAAAAHHHH, Aaaaaaaaaaaahhhh
My love did search
High and low
To find me here
Safe from woe
He soundly kissed

My parted lips
Long blue and cold
And now we hold
Each other's hand
And safely tread
Upon the land
Where snares nor foes
Can end our love
Until love's true kiss
In death.... we part
Now my love
Does waste away
In a small
Shallow grave
And love did fleet
As he sank so deep
And softly dreams
In death so sweet...
Aaaaaaaaahhhhhh, Aaaaaaaaaaahhhh
Aaaaaaaaahhhhhh, Aaaaaaaaaaahhhh

I FELT SO ENTRANCED with her song as I leaned in to kiss her lips smiling sweetly. I was jerked back at the last moment, landing on the ground below. My eyes instantly searched for

Luxina to see if she was harmed or safe when I came to realize a siren sat upon the river bend of the forge. I had been entranced by one of those cursed things Alpha's minions had created by mistake while goofing off with Seelie blood and demon blood. I glanced over my shoulder and was surprised to see Nautila standing behind me.

"Queen Mab should have known better than to send you into the Nightmares and Shadows realm alone. I'm surprised you aren't dead yet," Nautila hissed, pulling me to my feet. "Or perhaps that was her plan?" she asked, raising an accusing eyebrow.

"Nautila, what are you doing here?" I asked, bewildered to see a familiar face.

"It looks like I am saving you," she smirked. "That's what I am doing here."

"No, what are you doing in Nightmares and Shadows? How did you even find me?" I asked as we walked.

"My family is from this realm," she replied curtly. "I, however, found this place to be distasteful for my liking."

She handed me the map and the stone light that Nillona had given me.

"That still doesn't explain how you found me?" I asserted again.

"I ran across the Gwyllions' village. It's another quick way to get to the main city here, Caudir. That city is where the dark market is, and I do a lot of trading there. Nillona sent me in this direction, telling me you were probably already dead. For an angel, you sure can be tricked into illusions easily," she mused.

"Of course, her sending me this way was a trick. I should have known," I muttered, walking along with the map, seeing where we were.

The map had an ex on Bleeding Heart's Forge. "Oh, that explains everything," I hissed.

"Nillona did not send you here to trick you into death. If she wanted to kill you, she would have left you in the Bog of Damnation," Nautila replied. "You're headed in the right direction," she belted, annoyed as I watched the map and the path in front of me.

"Right direction to where?" I asked exhaustedly. "I don't even know where I am supposed to be going, let alone where I have been."

She smiled. "Silly, you are looking for the end of the shadowland. There will be an exit portal there that will take you wherever you wish to go. All you must do is think of the place or a person, and you are there."

"Well, that would have been nice information to know prior to being tossed in here," I replied, irritated. "Are those creatures still looking for me?" I asked as we walked.

"I have no idea," she answered. "They were gone from the Gwyllion village by the time I happened by."

"Were they able to ward them off?" I asked.

"Gwyllions are pretty adept at fighting off attacks," she replied. "Most of them were ok. There were just a few that didn't make it. There's a rule about fey. If they are attacked by an animal or attacked by a bug, they die from the interaction. Our bodies build a neurotoxin that kills us within a few hours. The poison is what killed them."

"It doesn't change the fact they were injured and put in harm's way due to trying to keep those monsters from mauling me. I hate knowing there are people dying for me," I admitted. "I don't deserve that. I am not worthy of that type of loyalty."

"You don't give yourself much credit, handsome," she teased.

I felt the heat rush to my cheeks. I wasn't used to that type of response by my body in the least. Insecurity was something new that I had to find a way to get around. I was not handsome in the least now, not with all these scars that riddled my face.

"Do you know the way to the portal without this map?" I asked her, changing the direction the conversation may have headed.

She shook her head. "You need that map because the portal is never in the same place for long. So, the map will lead you to it wherever its new resting place is for the day."

"Oh, that is just perfect!" I shouted sarcastically.

"Knowing my luck, one day I will be right near it, and the next it will be back where I started."

"Don't say such things of bad luck here, or they will manifest," she warned urgently. "This place makes your fears, anxieties, and nightmares come to life. It's why mostly fey travel these plains. We are pretty much joyous beings."

She frowned immediately after saying that, considering we were traveling beside a suicide river. She hooked her arm with mine as we continued to walk by the river.

"Don't look. Don't listen and act like the river doesn't exist," she urged. "Don't even look at the map to see where we are. Just keep your eyes on the road ahead of us."

"What is it?" I whispered. "It can't be worse than what I have already experienced. I was almost hanged at that tree."

"This is much worse, and as long as they don't catch your attention, it won't lure you in," she declared. "You don't want to know what it is, and it's best you remain in the unknown. You are far more susceptible to the temptation of this river."

"Why?" I asked.

"Do I really need to explain it to you?" she hissed. "It's called the River of Sorrows. You're not exactly a jovial person. You have too much darkness swirling within you."

So, for once, I listened, and I kept my eyes straight ahead and muted out the sounds of the world around me.

CHAPTER 9

WE HAD TRAVELED for what seemed like days. Nautila steered me clear of any of the enchanting elements that the shadowland possessed. We grew closer to the dark markets and cities of the shadows, and she indicated she knew a place where we could stay and get much needed sleep. I had never traveled through the Otherworld and witnessed their cities, villages, or markets. I had only ever been to the Unseelie Court Kingdom. There was nothing to compare to how the dark market operated here. However, I knew whatever they were doing wasn't allowable in any sense in either of the courts of the Otherworld. It also made me wonder what business Nautila would have had in the market. It couldn't be Mab approved, and if it was, what on earth would Mab desire to gain from a market she bans to other Unseelies for use.

It wasn't long after venturing into the dark market that my questions were answered. All around us, there were diverse types of vendors that sold unspeakable things. People bartered with enslaved fey here. Those from the Seelie court were of a higher price than those of the Unseelie court because of their pure blood. I saw exotic forms of food being cooked, sold, and served tableside at vendor shops. There were weapons shops, tailor shops, everything imaginable here.

"Do not make eye contact with any of the vendors here," Nautila warned, wrapping herself in a cloak and raising the hood over her head. "Not all fey here are as kind as Nillona was to you. Some of them would sell you to the highest bidder or worse, make a deal with Alpha for your head."

I nodded, acknowledging her warning as she handed me a cloak. I quickly put it on and kicked the hood up over my head. We maneuvered through the crowds with person after person bumping into us. I often caught stares from people who saw my face and flinched away from their view. I would tug the hood down further, but it kept sliding up. The deeper we moved into the crowd, the more the stares came to follow me across the courtyard as we walked.

"Ignore the sideways glances. You look fine," Nautila whispered, linking her arm with mine.

She tugged at me as we made it to a tavern. She pulled me through the doors and then scampered off to find the innkeeper. I stood near the door in a corner so as to not attract attention to myself until she returned with a key.

"They only had one room to share, so it looks like we are roomies tonight," she teased.

"Lead the way," I replied, holding my hand out in gesture.

She scrunched her face into a smile, grabbed my hand, and led me upstairs where the rooms were located. She found the door with our number on it, opened it, and stood aside for me to go in first. I brushed past her into the room. It had one bed, a table and chair on one wall, and a sofa couch against another wall. A small, curtained window was on the far side of the room that overlooked the market below. I briskly walked to the window and pulled the curtains shut so nobody could look into the window. She followed me into the room, closed the door, and slid the lock into place. She removed her cloak and set it on the chair. She fluffed her hair out as I slid my cloak off as well, tossing it on the couch. She stretched her arms out and stifled a yawn.

"You can have the bed," I offered. "I will take the couch."

"Now, that doesn't sound fun," she mumbled, puckering her bottom lip. "You can lie with me. I don't bite."

She climbed onto the bed and patted a spot beside her. My eyes trailed her body as they had the night in the Unseelie court room. I hesitated a moment before I relented and crawled in bed beside her. She let out a soft giggle of triumph. She propped herself up on her elbow and stared down at me.

"You're still a pure one, aren't you?" she asked teasingly.

"What do you mean pure?" I responded, not understanding the question.

"You've never been with a woman, have you?" she asked.

My face tightened in anger and humiliation. "That's really none of your concern or of importance at this moment," I retorted.

"Ah, so you haven't," she giggled. "That can change tonight if you want."

She went to touch my chest when I snatched her hand in midair.

"Not going to happen," I replied, standing up.

I moved over to the couch and sprawled out on it.

"She must be really special to you," she spoke softly.

"It has nothing to do with anyone else. I am simply not interested," I replied.

"Is it because I am a fey?" she demanded. "I can change my appearance for you. I can be whoever you want me to be."

I looked over as she began to transform into different women she must have come across paths with. Her final form landed on that of Luxina.

"Is that better?" she asked, her voice sounding just like Luxina's.

"You may be able to look like her, but you will never be able to be her," I declared.

"What makes her so much better than me?" Nautila demanded, shifting back into her own form.

"It's not that she is better than you. It's something you wouldn't understand," I stressed back.

"It's that stupid prophecy, isn't it? If not for that prophecy promising you to one another, you wouldn't think twice about her and would lie with me tonight," she insisted.

"If there wasn't a prophecy, I wouldn't even be here right now. I most likely wouldn't even exist," I muttered in return. "So, the prophecy is the last reason for me rebuking your advances. I am simply not interested."

She stood from the bed and huffed, left the room, and slammed the door behind her. It didn't bother me. I just hoped I hadn't hurt the poor girl's feelings. I was used to solitude and being alone. I think there was more than it having anything to do with Luxina. I don't like having company. I don't like to be bombarded with questions and jives. I sighed heavily, wondering what my refusal to be intimate with her would bring me eventually. Would she hand me over to someone who would sell me to Alpha? It was doubtful but also a very real possibility. She simply wouldn't understand why I refused her. Of course, it has absolutely nothing to do with her. She is beautiful, her body is objective, and she is as nice as they come, but that doesn't change the fact that I am hideous and a monster. What would she possibly want with me when she is gorgeous, and I am a disgusting looking thing?

I had my doubts that even Luxina would love me after everything I had done and how I look now. *A face only a mother could love...* Nillona was right. No one would love me. They would use me for their own pleasure and superficial gains, but at the end of the day, they wouldn't love me. They wouldn't be able to get past the outer shell to learn about what's inside of me. So, even though she made advances against me, Nautila only wants to take pleasure in relations with an angel. It has nothing to do with me as a person on the inside. It has to do with me being a powerful entity.

Nautila had been gone for quite some time. I was just about to go look for her when a commotion broke out on the other side of the window. I peeled myself from the couch and walked over, pulling back the curtains to peer out and see what was going on. Nautila burst through the door of the room with frightened, wide eyes.

"Demons are in the market looking for you," she blurted.

She ran to the window beside me, and we looked down at the groups of dark fey gathered as a handful of the sentinel demons of Alpha's army slowly walked through, surveying the vendors' tables. I watched as they looked around at their faces, removing the hoods of those that were cloaked. Dark fey stood frightened at their tables, unable to move or escape to somewhere safe. They tousled some of the dark fey around in the crowd until the streets began to clear out. They all piled into shops up and down the courtyard so they could escape from the Forsaken.

"We are looking for the Shining One," one of them bellowed. "We know he is here. We will leave everyone unharmed as long as he is turned over to us."

I watched, frowning as they moved table to

table, storefront to storefront. They weren't going to stop searching until I was found. There would only be bloodshed until I was turned over if they didn't get answers soon.

"What do you think they want with you?" Nautila whispered.

I dropped the curtain, stepped away from the window, and began to pace.

"I have no idea," I replied. "There could be a number of reasons. There was an uprising in the demonic ranks when I escaped. They could be either friendly or foes."

"I can find out for you," she mumbled.

"No, the best thing to do will be to wait it out until they leave," I remarked.

"What if they don't leave? What if they start killing fey one by one?" she asked.

"If they start doing that, then I will reveal myself. I won't let any more people die to save me," I hissed.

She watched me carefully. I'm not sure if she was reading into anything I said or trying to determine if I was really worth all the hassle of keeping safe. Either way, she climbed into her bed, and I followed suit, lying back down on the couch. I lay there sleepless for hours, just waiting for something to happen. I thought the door would bust open or something, and they would drag me to the courtyard to kill. Different scenarios played in my head until there was a thunderous sound outside. It was startling enough to wake Nautila from her sleep. We both slowly walked back to the window and peeked through the curtain to see what was happening in the marketplace.

"Damian!" one of the demons shouted. "We know you are here. It's time to show yourself, or these innocent fey will die one by one."

"It's a trick," Nautila refuted. "They won't hurt anyone."

She was interrupted as another thunderous sound rumbled through the courtyard. They were blowing up the shops one by one. I grabbed my weapons bag and tossed it over my shoulder, then picked up the cloak she had given me, tossing it over my back. I tied it and flipped the hood up.

"You stay here. Thank you for all you have done for me," I said as I opened the door to the room.

"I can help," Nautila replied. "I was trained to fight in battle. Queen Mab thought I was too pretty to fight, so ordered me to the castle."

"No," I replied. "This isn't your fight."

I left the room, closing the door behind me, and started my way down the steps. Dark fey lined the walls, watching me descend to the tavern below. No one spoke a word as I walked past each of them, but they did lower their heads in some form of respect. All these fey knew who I was and had refused to tell the demons where I was. I had to pay my gratitude and keep them from dying aimlessly for Alpha's stupid cause. I walked through the door of the tavern and out into the middle of the market. Dozens of dark fey parted ways for me to make it through the crowd and to those who were demanding my head on a platter.

"I'm here," I called out from the crowd, stepping out into the open space between the dark fey and the demons.

I looked from face to face at those who stood before me searching for me. I didn't recognize their faces, so I could only surmise they were not friendly but foes.

"Well, well, well," the ringleader spoke. "If it isn't the prodigal son."

"I'm sorry, have we met?" I asked.

"I am Raum, commander of 30 legions," he snarled.

"Oh, you must not be too important then. Those that Alpha takes council with I know personally," I jested. "So, obviously, you have no authority to demand my name in crowds without punishment."

"Because of you, thousands of demons have been pitted against one another. One side fighting for Alpha, and the other fighting for you. You are a poor excuse of existence, and it will be my privilege to kill you on sight as ordered by Alpha," he sneered, pulling a sword from the sheath on his side.

"You can try," I replied, arrogant and smiling.

I tore the hood from my head, unraveled the cloak from my body, and threw it on the ground beside me, wielding two large swords that I had activated while he was distracted talking. I spun the swords over the tops of my hands and readied them in combat stance.

"Are you sure you want to do this?" I asked.

He grinned deeply. "It will be my pleasure to be the one to rip your beating heart from your chest."

I leapt with agility and brought my swords down on him. I pushed him around the market with blow upon blow as I laid down an assault of weapon mastery. I saw the fear creep into his eyes as he parried and blocked as fast as he could.

"Alpha didn't tell you he was sending you to your death, did he?" I asked as I pounded him with blows. "I bet he also forgot to mention that I was trained by the best of the best for combat fighting, something even you are not entitled to."

My sword caught his arm, and he grabbed it with his free hand. I had him backed into a wall with no escape. The other demons that had been burning down the shops were now standing behind me as I held my sword to his throat.

"We can do this the easy way, or we can do it the hard way," I declared. "The uncomplicated way is you letting me go and living in the end without your buddies here dying along with you. You leave the shadows and report to Alpha, telling him you found nothing here. The hard way is I kill you and then take out those standing behind me. Alpha still doesn't know I have been found, and these hospitable dark fey will still be safe and sound from future attacks."

He laughed. "You will never be able to run and hide from Alpha. He owns you!" he sneered.

"Last chance," I replied through gritted teeth. "What's it going to be, boys?"

I looked back at those who stood behind me. A couple of faces looked back and forth between one another nervously but still held their swords ready for attack.

"The hard way it is," I sneered.

Raum pushed me off and sliced his blade through the air. I ducked and twisted around, my foot catching his feet and taking him down to the ground. I brought my sword up and over my head and crashed it down on his neck. His head rolled for about five feet before it stopped, his hollow dead eyes staring back at me. I turned my head to the others and glared. At some point, you would think stupidity would disappear and be replaced by fear. These idiots were not the case. They lunged toward me. I picked my swords up and fought them off. One sword parried and blocked one of them while the other sword concentrated on the other. I kicked out with my foot, catching one behind me in the chest and knocking him to the ground.

"That's enough!" a voice yelled.

We all stopped to look at the one who had shouted for our attention. One of the demons had slipped off when I wasn't watching and had Nautila with a sword at her throat. I glared at him as he brought it up closer to her neck. Her eyes widened with fear.

"She's not part of this," I growled. "She is just an innocent fey like everyone standing in this marketplace. Your fight and qualm are with me. Let her go."

"Ah, you see, this one has a thing for you, though," the demon replied, sniffing her hair deeply. "I heard her telling the girls in the tavern that she had planned to get you as hers one way or another."

"She is still innocent and not worth killing for me," I protested angrily. "I am not worthy of bloodshed. Why do you lay down your lives for Alpha when he sent you here to die!?" I bellowed. "Are you that blind? Do you not know when he is sacrificing you, or are you too bloodthirsty to realize you are being used?"

"I sacrifice myself in the name of Alpha as all his army should," he testified.

"That is such a shame," I maintained. "If you can take me alive or dead, you can try. But, let her go.

She has no part of this."

"Soft on this one, aren't you?" he jeered, grabbing her by her jowls.

"I just don't want people dying for me," I replied.

"You should have thought about that when you were Alpha's little minion," he seethed. "Her blood is on your hands."

He swiped the sword across Nautila's throat, and she choked, gasping for air as her mouth filled with blood. She thudded to the ground, eyes wide open and blood leaking from the corner of her lips. Anger tore through me.

"I suggest any other fey that is willing to aid the Shining One go quietly inside," the demon spoke aloud.

They didn't spare a moment and clamored as quickly as they could from the marketplace back into the shops that weren't burned down.

"What's your name?" I muttered.

"What?" he asked, confused.

"What is your name?" I annunciated.

"Zepar," he replied. "But why do you want to know?"

"Because I want to know what to carve in your dead body as I send it back to Alpha with a message," I sneered.

I held my swords out and spun around quickly, dispatching the three demons who had stood around me earlier, fighting. Their heads rolled across the ground landing at Zepar's feet as their bodies thumped to the ground.

"Alpha won't stop with us. He will just keep sending more of us to find you," Zepar laughed. "Kill us. Kill one, and two shall rise in his place," he hissed.

"Well, then I guess I will just kill all of you until there is no one left but Alpha," I remarked, swinging my sword around, preparing it for my assault on his body.

"You can take us out, but you will never defeat what he created just for you," Zepar replied. "You will not live to see the end of the world."

He blew a whistle in the air as I ran toward him, bringing my blade up and over my head, slicing it down the middle of his body. He crumpled in halves to the ground, blood spraying me as he fell. I lifted Nautila's body from the ground and carried her to the tavern door, laying her gently down. She shouldn't have died. Her death was now on my own hands. Even if I hadn't been the one to take her life, she was killed because of me.

The dark fey began to pour out from the shops they had taken refuge in and stood around me in a circle.

"You are the brave Shining One who everyone has been talking about," one of them asserted.

I nodded my head.

"We will stand by your side," he replied, putting his arm across the middle of his chest. "The dark fey will fight your fight. Alpha will pay for his crimes against all fey."

They all stood around me, each placing their arm over their chest and bowing to me. I bowed my head in acknowledgement of their loyalty.

"Damian!" a familiar voice shouted through the crowd.

I looked around, and my eyes landed on another fleet of demons who were heading into the market square. I searched the faces to match the voice I had heard call my name, and my eyes stopped on the face of Asmodeus. The dark fey stood around me and readied whatever weapons they had on their sides to fight against the new wave of demons advancing. I motioned for them to lower their weapons.

"Asmodeus," I replied, walking up to him.

I kept my distance, unsure of whether he had finally turned against me and was here to drag me back to Alpha or not. I didn't have to give it much thought as he wrapped his arms around me in a bear hug.

"You are a sight for sore eyes," he murmured. "I was afraid we wouldn't get here in time to stop Zepar and Raum's gang."

His eyes rested on the bodies of the demons lying on the ground. He cocked an eyebrow.

"I was trained by the best," I replied with a

shrug.

"Well, they were the least of your problems. Those things Alpha created are on their way here. Zepar released the call to signal where you are," he replied.

"We must leave here, then. These fey do not deserve to die," I said.

I turned around to all those who stood behind me. "Seek shelter. Lock your doors, bolt them, and make sure they are impenetrable. There are far more things to fear than the shadows here, and those things are on their way to this very place. So, go. Hide!" I instructed them.

They nodded and began to file away into the shops quietly. I returned my attention to Asmodeus and those who stood behind him. "You all need to leave as well. These things... they are unlike anything of Alpha's I have fought."

"No," Asmodeus protested. "This is the one time we will not listen to you. We will stay, and we will fight them alongside you. And if we die, then so be it. But you will not face them alone anymore. Half of the demons split in two. Those that side with Alpha, and those that side with you. We plan to meet up with Incaendiel and the rest of the angels to join forces."

"So, he is, ok?" I asked. "Incaendiel?"

"As far as I know, he is. I haven't heard if he has

been recaptured or not," Asmodeus replied.

"And my- I mean Sophie?" I asked.

He shook his head. "Sophie is a lost cause to all but Incaendiel."

A howl ripped through the air, jerking us away from our conversation. Those that stood with me all faced the other direction. We all readied our weapons, waiting for the beasts to rip through the courtyard. The sounds seemed to come from all sides as we all followed the sounds, turning around and around as the creatures circled the market, ensuring none of us escaped.

"You ready?" Asmodeus asked, scanning the openings between all the buildings that stood around us.

"Are you?" I answered.

Werewolves burst through the buildings, snapping, snarling, and growling. Their fangs dripped the same acid that those from the gladiator ring did. The fighting began. The sounds of swords ripping through flesh and howls of pain filled the air around us as we tore and hacked our way through the ferocious group of beasts. However, no matter how many of them we slaughtered, more poured in around us.

I caught notice of several types of creatures making their way into the market square. They were all the same ones that I had watched emerge from the tunnels prior to Incaendiel yanking me behind the gate. None of us would make it out of this alive, that was for sure. We were outnumbered by thousands. I looked around at those who stood by my side, fighting. They fought with me, for me, and because of me, and if they had a choice, they would die with me. I would never let them do that, though. I am not worth the lives of others and never would be.

Arrows tore through the sky, catching the creatures left and right squarely in the center of their heads. They dropped like flies one by one as mountains and mountains of arrows rained down around us. Some were fiery arrows, while others exploded upon contact. I looked to the tops of the buildings, and the dark fey who had hidden away in their buildings stood on the building tops, aiding us in the fight. Fireballs were flung from catapults, exploding in molten lava balls burning the creatures to a crisp. Bombs were released that, upon impact, poisonous gas crept upon the beasts, and they gasped, dropping to the ground hacking and frothing at the mouth.

Cries and shouts erupted from the building tops as the dark fey began to be attacked by creatures that flew. The winged beasts flew around, snatching them from the buildings, ripping them apart in the air, and tossing the carcasses to the ground below. I used my icy powers and began to shoot ice spears through the air taking them down one by one as those who were able to use their own arrows to take them out of the sky.

"We need to get you out of here!" Asmodeus shouted, fending off attacks from his left and right.

"I can't leave them behind defenseless," I replied, turning my ice powers to those who were on the ground.

One of the creatures shot out a flaming torch of breath that I quickly threw up an ice shield against. The ice slowly melted from around us as more and more of them appeared, breathing fire.

"When are you going to get it through your head that without you, there is no end to Alpha?" Asmodeus hissed. "Now, you need to get out of here while we hold them off. We have enough assistance from the dark fey to keep them from following you."

"Where am I supposed to go!?" I shouted. "Do I just appear out of thin air to Luxina and Xavier and expect them to welcome me with open arms?"

"You have to do what you have to do!" he yelled. "They will know. I am sure the message has been gotten out to them. They have a fey with them who has been helping them. She must know something about what is happening. The entire universe is buzzing about it! Everyone is antsy and can feel the war brewing like a storm."

"I left you behind once," I replied. "I won't leave you behind with certain death."

"You've been like a son to me," Asmodeus

173

replied, placing his forehead against me. "And I would rather nothing more than to die protecting you as such."

"Why does everyone I care about have to die for me?" I protested. "This shouldn't be the way things are!"

"Things don't always work out as we hope," Asmodeus replied quietly. "But we must push forward with what we are given. I was once an angel that darkness stole. I won't let that same darkness take you and claim you. Now, go! Run! And don't stop running for anyone until you get to where you need to be."

"And where is it I need to be?" I replied, refusing to accept his words. "What if I belong nowhere?"

"You belong!" he yelled. "You belong! Don't ever let anyone make you think that you aren't worthy of respite, or worthy of love, or worthy of existence. You don't let anyone tell you that you are a monster! You aren't a monster! And you deserve the light more than most of us ever have!"

He pushed me from the center of the fleet toward an opening that was free from any of the creatures.

"Go, Damian!" he shouted. "I will see you again."

I backed away slowly, still unsure if I should leave them. I couldn't leave them. I couldn't leave

Asmodeus to die. I couldn't, and I wouldn't. I summoned my power from deep within, and ice rained in sheets from the skies, driving the Forsaken helping me further back to the buildings. They had to duck inside and take cover from the assault of daggers that fell from the sky. I screamed. I howled in anger. Power exploded from my core, and blue lights swirled around the square as torrential freezing winds swarmed the creatures. The lights swirled around them as they began to gasp and choke, starved of air.

No sooner had the beasts collapsed to the ground, suffocated, more creatures began to pour into the square. I could fight them all day like this. I planted my feet, preparing for the onslaught, when a yell erupted throughout the rumble of monsters.

"Damian! Go!" Asmodeus bellowed.

I scowled in frustration. I gave a quick look at the creatures and then to Asmodeus. He and the other demons stepped out in front of them as they rushed to the center of the marketplace, and they began fighting the beasts off for me to escape. I turned and ran through the opening that still remained free from the growing carnage. I slipped through the alleyway between the buildings and ran off into the shadows as they rapidly overtook me, encasing me in a shroud of inky black protection.

CHAPTER 10

I STILL HAD THE MAP and pulled it from the bag around my shoulder. I picked up the stone, and it lit up in my hand, illuminating the area around me as I walked. It was nothing but the road I had been on for miles. I looked at the map, and it told me where I was located. *Wandering Road* was what it showed to me.

"Great," I muttered to myself. "I bet this road makes me walk and walk without ever reaching my destination. Another cruel joke from the realm."

I quickly scanned the map to see if I was close to the portal. To my luck, I was close. If I didn't get lost by following this road, then I would make it there within a few hours. However, the tricky nature of this place was sure to slow me down for sure. I just hoped I would reach the portal before it jumped to another place. I was tired of traveling. I was more than tired. My heart, body, and soul were exhausted from this place, exhausted from the predicament I had come to find myself in. I was ready for it all to be over with.

If this was what mortals believed hell to be like, I would quickly agree. This place was worse than Sheol. I had always found it amusing how the mortals stuck to their beliefs of eternal fires and damnation when no such place had ever existed. The Lake of Fire spoken of in their written texts was an illusion that Alpha had created. Quite honestly, there was no such place as heaven either. There was no eternal resting place in the sky where you got to sit with God at his throne. Much like death for angels, mortals just dissipated into the universe and released their energies back to it. The Summit may be quite like what they believed heaven to be, but it was solely the home for angels.

What mortals didn't understand about their god, about Alpha, was that he didn't care about anything but for them to worship him endlessly. That was the only thing Alpha wanted for everything he had created, which was for it to worship him. Nature, angels, mortals, and even those vile beasts, his only wish was for them to bow to his power. I remember the days we sat in the Summit and watched the mounting war between the angels of the Summit and those that had fallen to the Glade. Alpha enjoyed the negative energy he had sparked between them all. However, he despised Incaendiel for his lack of worship. For even as the Fallen Ones fought heavily against the angels of the Summit, they still loved their father creator. All of them loved Alpha except for Incaendiel. He had grown a hateful disposition toward Alpha that developed a depth no other had.

Mortals had called this adversary Lucifer. There was a story where God had asked him to love mortals more than he loved God and Lucifer refused. That's not what happened at all. We all knew that Omega was the one that chose to fall, and we all knew Incaendiel was the true adversary of Alpha. It was quite humorous knowing that he was created to take over power once Alpha and Omega grew powerless and turned back into stardust. He would win in the end, whether Alpha liked it or not. Incaendiel was the rightful god over the galaxy. He wouldn't be as conceited about it either.

I watched my footsteps appear on the map as I continued walking down the road. This contraption was unique and very handy. It was too bad that it only worked for the Nightmares and Shadows realm. It would prove to be quite useful elsewhere, like searching for Starfire. I let my thoughts drift to Luxina, and I wondered where they were at this very moment. Were they safe? Were they fighting off monsters as well?

Everything seemed to become a deafening silence around me. I hadn't even realized I wasn't making any noise as I trudged along the path. My feet fell silent against the road no matter how hard I stomped them. I stopped for a moment, looking in both directions of the road. I listened intently for any type of sound. The paper map in my hand didn't even make a noise as I rustled it. Something was off. Why were there no sounds here? I looked at the map to see if the name of the road had changed. I panicked slightly. There wasn't anything on the map at all. It was just a blank sheet of paper.

I folded it in half and then opened it again to see if there would be any change on it at all. There was nothing. There was no red x marking where I was on the map. There weren't any places listed, no forests, no red dots of where I had traveled from and toward. It was as if I had walked into a part of this place that didn't even exist in the land. I didn't know what to do. Do I keep walking and hope that the map reappears? Should I turn around and go back the way I came and hope that the map comes back? There were so many options and so few right answers as to what I should do.

I sat down in the middle of the road in defeat. Even if I traveled back the way I came, there was no guarantee I wouldn't become even more lost than I am right now. The road was called the *Wandering Road* for a reason. You wandered lost on it. If I stayed right here, maybe someone would happen along and tell me where I was and what I had to do to get back on course to my destination.

I lay down in the dirt and stared up at the dark sky where meteors had begun to fall again. They were beautiful streaks of pinks, purples, and blues. Even though this place was a black hole, it did have some beauty to it. Even the *River of Sorrows* had an elegance to it. Even though it was a heartbreaking place of fey suicides, it still had a beautiful symbolic meaning behind it. No one escapes the throes of death, and fey live for hundreds of years. Sometimes, suicide may seem like the only answer they have for escape. The spirits there showed they gained a semblance of peace because they did not reincarnate back into a young fey again. They were stuck in a limbo type state of being without having to experience life all over through another set of eyes.

Maybe that is what it would be like for me. If I were to die, I don't think I would drift off to the land of the fallen angels at Potter's Field. I believe that just like the gods releasing their energies back into the world, I would, too. I would float through the universe endlessly as stardust until it was used to mold another being. Maybe the stardust would have some sort of conscience like most believed souls to have. Would I float around like a spirit in the vapid space of the universe? Mysteries of death have always captivated me.

My mind soon replayed the day over, and I was now thinking of Nautila. She was another person who died innocently because of me. If I had let her come with me to fight, would she still be alive instead of being caught off guard and dragged outside by Zepar? She hadn't even fought back with him even though she had said she was trained. Did she act as a martyr and let her death fuel the dark fey into joining the war? They had pledged their loyalty quickly after I had avenged her death. Could they see that I was compassionate?

As always, my thoughts drifted off to Luxina. I wanted to see her, to hear her voice. I wanted to know she was protected and that whoever protected her would swear her life over theirs. That was the type of protection she needed. All these people were dying for me, and I wasn't worthy of such selfless acts. But she was. She deserved people to die to protect her. I need to be there to protect her. I needed to make sure these creatures would never hurt her. How do I get to her, though? I sighed deeply. I closed my eyes and pictured her face in my head. Her red, fiery hair wrapped around her face where her green eyes shined back brightly at me.

The sounds of crickets filled my ears, and I opened my eyes to see if there was something growing closer to me on this road. My eyes looked directly up into the night sky where stars shone brightly, and a full moon hovered just above the canopy of treetops. I sat up, looked around me, and saw that I was in a thicket of bushes. I pulled the map out that I had tucked away to see where I was at in Nightmare and Shadows. How did I move when I didn't move at all? When I pulled the map out, the red x was back, and I was somewhere in a place called The Netherlands. I stood up and scratched my head. This was a map of places on Earth. I glanced back and forth where I stood, and sure enough, I was surrounded by regular trees and growing foliage.

"I must have walked into the portal and didn't even know it," I murmured to myself. "But why am I here?"

I heard voices off from where I stood and quickly squatted in the brush so I wouldn't be seen by whoever was walking toward me. It could be anyone at this point. I focused on the thoughts of the people who were advancing toward me.

What does she want now? I heard in my head. *I wish she would just leave me alone. She always wants to talk. I don't have anything to say to her. People seem to die around us all the time. We aren't worth it. She just keeps pushing on.*

Is that Xavier? I tried to peer through the brush to get a look at who I was hearing in my head.

If I must hear any more about the need to save Damian from Alpha, I will rip my ears from my head. It's always Damian this and Damian that. Then, she wonders why I am in a bad mood. Maybe if she cared more about me than she did him, she would see the pain that I am in as well. She is so self-centered.

They were within range of me to hear the spoken conversation they were having.

"Did I make you mad at me or something? It's been a year of these conversations," she asked Xavier.

I could feel the pain and torment that she felt regarding him. He must have been pushing her away for quite some time, jealous over me. So, the Unseelies did not lie when I was told that she wanted to find me.

"You didn't do anything," he replied heatedly. "I just don't want to talk."

I watched as he walked away through the trees back to wherever they had come from. How could he leave her there alone and in such pain? I watched as she fought back the tears threatening to spill down her face. I imagined what it would feel like to brush the tears away while caressing her face in my hands.

I stepped out from the brush without thinking. My heart raced, and my mouth went dry. I needed to let her know I was here. I needed to comfort her. I needed to take her fears away. But most of all, I needed to protect her.

"Give him time, Luxina," I spoke softly into the night air.

Her eyes landed on me, and I could see and hear all the questions that bubbled beneath her surface. Deep within those questions, I felt what I needed to feel from her. It might seem trivial to most that I needed this type of response to know that I was accepted by her and possibly even quite loved. But it was the most soothing experience my weary soul could feel after my travels. After experiencing everything I had felt in the realm of Nightmares and Shadows. What the *Bog of Damnation* and the *River of Sorrows* had put me through regarding my growing love for her. I felt her heart flutter...

Sneak Peek of *The Valley of the Shadow of Death: Nephilim Rising,* Book 4 in the Guardians of Light Series

PROLOGUE

IT HAD BEEN A YEAR since we escaped Alpha. Xavier and I hid in the realms of the Otherworld as we made our journey to find Starfire. Praeziel was our guide, along with Gwendolyn, as we hopped from portal to portal, trying to find the oracle's cloaked cabin. We have traveled far and wide, often crossing the same places twice, looking for her. By the time we had reached her last known place of existence, she had already fled to seek safety and refuge from Alpha. My understanding has been that Alpha knows about her and has for quite some time. It has been his plan to find her so she can help him with Damian like she is to help us.

Praeziel doesn't know much about how she is going to help us. The only thing he knows is that she is the key to unlocking our full potential. My guess is that it has to do with the faery enchantment that was placed upon our parents when they were created.

I find myself every day wondering if my parents are both okay and if Damian is being tortured anymore. We know for a fact that Alpha is still running tests and creating new species of demons. We have happened across a few of them along our travels that we had to dispatch. Damian's altered blood is now the key to these creatures, whether Alpha has perfected his serum or not. After my visions with the injections, everyone began to wonder if my mother, Sophie, had actually died or not when the Glade fell to ruin.

After we visit with Starfire, that is when the real battle of minds and wits begins. Alongside Praeziel, we will have to convince the Nephilim to join ranks with us to help defeat Alpha. We gained alliances with Seelies and Unseelies and even mended the bonds of discrimination amongst their ranks. A new world order is coming to pass, but only if we are able to defeat Alpha in the end. If we can stave off the apocalypse that is brewing, ending the heavenly war, we will, without a doubt, be able to forge an unbreakable alliance to keep the Children of the Night and the Forsaken in the abyss with all of the other monsters Alpha created throughout time.

CHAPTER 1

"WHERE COULD SHE BE?" I asked as I loaded my arms with firewood.

Xavier and Praeziel had been slowly building us a fire for the night with what sticks we could scrounge up from the area. I dropped the firewood beside their circle of stones and dusted my hands off on my pants. A chill had filled the air, and I rubbed my arms. We were far from any trail in a remote area of the wooded hills in Europe. We had traveled through so many faery portals that I didn't even know which country we were in this time. Gwendolyn had gone to hunt us some food to roast over the fire and hadn't made it back yet. It made me nervous whenever she went off by herself. We could be ambushed at any moment of the day, and we are better in numbers. Xavier and I were the only safe ones from harm. Alpha would have

Praeziel and Gwendolyn killed on-site. I couldn't live with myself knowing more people had died trying to keep us safe from Alpha.

"Gwendolyn not only goes out to hunt but to ask local fey if they have heard of anything from the trees, plants, or animals as to where she may have gone," Praeziel replied, jabbing a stick into the fire and kindling it into a roar.

"I wonder if we keep tripping her senses, and she believes we are the danger that Alpha poses," I commented, hunching down beside the warm flames.

"That could very well be," Praeziel replied, leaning back against a tree stump.

Xavier sat quietly, picking at blades of grass, lost in thought. If only I knew what went through his mind… somehow, he was able to put a block up so I couldn't hear his thoughts anymore. It happened after the escape from Stygia. I'm sure it had to do with meeting our father for the first time. Or maybe learning his mother had died. Actually, it could be a number of things, but it doesn't make the loneliness I feel any better.

"I'll take first watch tonight," Praeziel stated as he watched me yawn.

"Oh, I'm not even tired. I'm just cold," I replied with an appreciative smile, rubbing my arms again.

"I don't ever recall being this cold. Where are we?" I asked.

"We are in the Netherlands," Gwendolyn replied, appearing with rabbits, squirrels, and some bird attached to strings slung over her shoulder. Her hunting bowstring rested across her chest with her quivers on the opposite shoulder, along with the prey she had hunted.

"Any word?" Praeziel asked.

"Possibly," she replied as she plopped the dead animals down in front of her. She pulled out a blade and began to skin the animals to prepare them for the fire. "I spoke with some of the river nymphs, and they heard tale that Starfire is on an island out past Australia. It's a few days' journey from here."

"That's good news, right?" I asked, looking between her and Praeziel.

They both nodded quietly and returned to the silence of the night. Xavier didn't make a sound nor acknowledge Gwendolyn's return. I could watch the air around him darken and shroud him as he thought deeper and deeper to himself.

"Xavier," I spoke aloud. He glanced up to me, bewildered, looking around. "Let's go for a walk," I said with a small smile.

"Don't stray too far," Gwendolyn ordered. "The hills around here are treacherous, and you could find yourself in a hole made by trappers."

"We'll be careful," I promised as I stood up and held my hand out to Xavier to take.

He stood along with me and walked over to me, but he didn't take my hand. His demeanor toward me had changed ever since we went to see the Dark Queen. He hardly talked to me anymore. He never held me while we slept, and any type of physical contact was put to the back of his mind. I don't know what I did to make him angry with me or to change in regards to me, but a sinking feeling always blossomed in my bosom whenever he refused my hand.

"A penny for your thoughts," I said, as we strolled silently through the trees.

He still didn't speak, and I sighed. "What's wrong, Xavier? You never talk to me anymore. What's going on in that head of yours?" I asked, peering up at him in the little bit of moonlight that breached the tops of the trees.

"I just don't have anything to say," he replied.

"Did I make you mad at me or something? It's been a year of these conversations," I asked, prodding deeper.

"You didn't do anything," he replied heatedly. "I just don't want to talk."

And with that, he stalked off back the way we came to the campsite and left me alone in the dark.

Tears threatened to spill as I once again felt as if my heart was going to break in two.

"Give him time, Luxina," the voice called out in the dark.

I jerked my head around, trying to scan anywhere I could see in the dark. I knew that voice. Only one person would call me sister. Damian. But how did he find us?

"How would I not find you? You're my blood," the reply came to the silent question in my head.

I still couldn't find him in the dark, inky black of night. Was he here to steal me back away to Alpha? Was he here to kill me as he had killed Sophia?

"No and no," he replied.

I heard a twig snap, and I jerked my head in the direction it came from. There, in the low glow of the moon, I saw the red curls split through the dark trees. I was too far from the campsite to yell for help even if he did intend to hurt me. I had no weapons on me, either.

"I can sense your fear and anxiety. I assure you, sister, that I am not here to hurt you. As a matter of fact, I am here to help you put an end to Alpha's reign of terror," Damian said as he stepped into the light, and I could see his face.

I scanned it deeply, looking for a twitch or a tell-tale sign of him lying. I didn't find anything. My insides wrenched against each other as I grappled with my own fears. Could I trust him? And even though the past could clearly show I could not, something tugged at me as my heart thumped that said I could indeed trust him.

"Were you followed?" I asked, scanning the area from where he appeared in the dark.

"No. I slipped out undetected, and I am cloaked. No one, not even Alpha himself, would be able to find me by tracking my wings."

He stopped short of me with his hands clasped behind his back. I wonder if he has a weapon? As if to answer the question in my mind, he brought his hands around and showed they were indeed empty.

"I don't want to be Alpha's soldier any more than your father did," Damian stated, staring into my eyes. "I just want to be with those I care about. Not with someone who just uses me because I have special blood."

Funny enough, I believed every word he said. Even so, I had to be hesitant. I had to be sure.

"You killed Sophia. You killed Praeziel's mother," I said dryly.

"No, I did not. Sophia is safe and hidden away. I pretended to murder her to satisfy Alpha. Trust me, Luxina, she is safe and well with the Watchers that are left," he replied quietly. A few moments passed as I just stared him in the eyes. "You believe me, don't you?"

His voice was different from most of the times we talked. He sounded needy, as a child looking for approval from a parent would sound. The harsh undertones in his speech had filtered away, and a soft tone had replaced the voice of the boy that stole me away from my father. I took a deep breath and let my gut take control… or was it my heart?

"Oddly, yes. I believe you," I replied, stepping toward him. I reached my arms out to hug him, and he flinched away. I could see the terror in his eyes.

"I just want to hug you."

"Why?" he asked, looking closely at my hands, examining them for weapons.

"Because that's what people do when they care about one another," I replied as I wrapped my arms around his shoulders.

He didn't know what to do. I could tell he had never been shown affection by Alpha. He hesitated as he lifted his arms and placed them around my shoulders as well. The hug deepened, and his arms tightened around me as tears slid down his cheeks.

"I always knew you were in there, somewhere," I said as he silently sobbed into my hair.

"Alpha is so close to making the injections the right way, and I am so scared of the monster I would turn into," he cried out in breaths.

"We won't let that happen," Praeziel said, startling Damian and me from the hug.

Behind me stood Gwendolyn, Praeziel, and Xavier. I don't know how long they had been there watching. I didn't even hear them walk up. I am horrible at this whole stealth and hunting thing. Damian quickly swiped at his face, drying the tears so no one would see them.

"So, everyone is in agreement that Damian stays with us?" I asked, looking face to face.

Gwendolyn and Praeziel nodded. Xavier didn't even acknowledge the question. He just stared angrily at Damian and me. He scowled and stalked off back to the campsite alone.

"I will talk to him," Praeziel stated and sighed, heading back to the campsite as well.

"Good luck," I mumbled.

"As I said," Damian began. "Give him time."

"Easy for you to say. You haven't gotten the cold shoulder for a year now," I replied, more heated than intended. "Sorry. It just annoys me how he is acting so childish."

"He has every right to act childish," Damian replied softly and wisely. "He just lost his mother, and he doesn't know where his father is. There's more, but it's his business to bring it to light, not mine."

"The mother part, maybe. The father part, not so much. The first time he met Dad, all he did was sit and talk angrily, then glare at him. He blames everyone for growing up without a family to call his own," I said as we meandered back to the campsite.

"Don't we all," Damian whispered in reply.

I felt a pang of guilt. He and Xavier were alike. Neither grew up with their mother nor father. One grew up with Lilith, and the other grew up with Alpha. They were closer to being twins together than Xavier and I were.

"Well, I am here now. I will always be here," I replied as I took his hand in mine almost as if by instinct. "And when this is all over, you can live with us. My dad would love you as his own. You know that, right?"

He chuckled a bit. "Oddly enough, yes. I do know."

I squinted at him, wondering exactly what that meant. The last I knew of him meeting my father was the day he kidnapped me for Alpha. Based on that alone, there was no way my father would adore him, as I had stated, without getting to know the real him first. I mulled on it and let it go without prodding him further. By the time we had made it back to the campsite, Gwendolyn had the food roasting across the fire, Praeziel was watching the perimeter, and Xavier was sitting alone at a tree away from the fire. Damian dropped a bag at the tree line and took a seat near me at the fire.

"Dinner is almost ready," Gwendolyn stated, pinching the animals as they roasted. "You hungry?" she asked, looking at Damian.

A frown quickly hid the developing look of shock Gwendolyn had as she averted her eyes and looked back to the fire. I followed her gaze, looking at Damian more carefully. I nearly gasped. He was just skin and bones. Red scars littered his face as if he had been beaten with a whip. His eyes sunk in with black rings underneath them. Anger coursed through me, and steam began to rise from my skin. Damian stepped back, confused as to what he did wrong to spark such a response from me. A quick glance around the fire alluded him to the answer when no one would look directly at him. Once he realized it, he smirked a bit.

"To say I'm starving would be a bit of an understatement," he replied with a laugh.

The tension in the circle broke, and sympathy washed around everyone. I had recalled my fire back within before I burned the trees down around us. I had gotten better at controlling it with the help of Gwendolyn and Praeziel. They taught me a few calming tricks. Dad had always tried to help me, but he never could get it right. He still had troubles himself reeling in his own fire. I guess we all just had a temper with a short fuse, which is why.

Gwendolyn picked up one of the sticks that had a roasted rabbit on it and handed it over to Damian.

"Thank you," he replied as he took the stick from her.

Hungry eyes stared at the food, but his face also looked a shade of green as if the thought of food was revolting. That could be a very real possibility. I know they taught us in physical education that when the body is starved, food can make you sick.

"Take it one bite at a time," I coaxed.

He looked at me, and for the first time, the strong eyes I remembered seeing for the first time a year ago had disappeared. Before me sat a boy with puppy dog eyes, hoping that his weakness didn't make him actually weak.

"Luxina, here you go," Gwendolyn said, holding out a stick with a bird roasted on it.

"Thank you," I replied with a smile and glanced over to Xavier. "Hungry, X?" I asked.

He didn't answer me. I rolled my eyes as Gwendolyn reached over to him a stick with a squirrel on it, and he took it without offering a thank you or anything. I felt a hand brush my shoulder and knew it was Damian, reminding me again to give him time. Something tugged at my heart, and I brushed the feeling away. I stole glances at Damian as he took small bites of the food he was given. He had only eaten a small portion of the rabbit when he set it aside, propping it up against a tree, so he didn't get it dirty.

The circle was silent as everyone ate but didn't ask the lingering question in the air.

"How did I get away from Alpha?" Damian asked aloud. He smiled and chuckled a bit as we all looked a bit confused at him. "That answer is simple." He stood from his spot and stretched out his cramped legs and arms in the air before returning to his seated position. "Incaendiel helped me escape."

We all gawked at him. The question we had needed an answer to, and we finally received it. Alpha did have him. That's why he hadn't come for me.

"Is he ok?" I asked a bit too eagerly.

"He's alive." Damian wouldn't look at me. It was all the answer I needed. He may be alive, but he wasn't ok in the least bit of sense. "Alpha won't kill him. Trust me. Lucifer has tried to persuade him to let him perform the deed. He needs all of us," Damian replied. "And as for the mind-reading, no, it isn't your imaginations. I can read everyone's mind sitting around this campfire."

I glanced at Xavier to see if that bothered him. If it did, it didn't register with him. He sat silently, eating the food Gwendolyn had given him. He tossed the finished carcass off into the tree line, fixed his sleeping gear on the ground, and rolled over to go to sleep.

"I think Xavier has the right idea," Gwendolyn purred. "We should all get some rest."

"I have the first watch," Praeziel replied with a smile. "I called it already."

I had an extra bag with sleep gear in it that I had been toting in case one of ours was damaged in some way, so I tossed it over to Damian. He caught it and nodded his thanks. I put my sleeping bag on the ground where I had been sitting, unzipped it, climbed inside of it, and zipped myself back up in it. The warmth of the bag enveloped me, and I snuggled deeper down into it. Damian stretched his out right above my head and just sat on top of it. His eyes looked so sunken in with the little light the glow of the fire emitted.

"How long has it been since you slept?" I asked, propping my head in my hand.

"Who says I sleep?" he chided.

"Because you are one of us. You sleep and most likely have dreams as well," I replied softly.

He was quiet for a few minutes. I sighed in exasperation. Looks like they both will only let me in so far. I rolled onto my back and stared at what few stars I could see through the canopy. I often wondered what the universe looked like from the gates of the Summit. I bet it was breathtaking. The beautiful lights of the stars dancing throughout the galaxy. The purple and pink particle clouds floating through space while comets shoot by.

"It is just that beautiful," Damian said, breaking me from my thoughts. "And I haven't slept in weeks, months before that. Not since Alpha began the torture…"

And it was back to silence. I didn't know what to say. I could only imagine what they had done to him. His own father… I drifted off to sleep with everything tumbling through my head. Damian was here. Damian was here safely. My father helped him escape. Alpha torturing him. What was he trying to get out of him? Did he know where we were, and Alpha knew? Was that what Alpha wanted from him? Maybe he stopped taking his injections.

Kasey Hill has lived in Franklin County, VA, for most of her adult life and is a versatile writer known for her work in several genres, including urban fantasy, horror, thriller, paranormal romance, and metaphysical/New Age topics. She has authored both fiction and non-fiction, with a particular interest in Wicca, specializing in Trinitarian Wicca as the historical archivist with an upcoming historical account of the shift from polytheism to monotheism in Abrahamic religions, where she has published non-fiction works exploring the subject.

Her fiction often dives into the supernatural and the macabre, blending mythological elements with modern storytelling. She has published multiple novels, poetry collections, and short stories. Notable works include her *Guardians of Light* series in the mythology fantasy genre, and her poetry that has received recognition for its depth and emotional resonance. As she grows in the horror genre, she has a particular penchant for Southern Gothic storytelling, such as her Adult Horror novel *Devil's Claw* and her Young Adult horror series, *The Whispering Spirits* featuring *The Haunting at Foxwood Village* and *Dark Coven*. She has several Horror short stories circulating for anthologies and Ezines featuring her unique style of worldbuilding.

In addition to her writing, Kasey Hill has also contributed to the Wiccan and occult community through her non-fiction work, making her a multi-faceted author with a broad range of interests and expertise.